# The Broken Hedge

## SHORT STORIES

### BY

### OCHUWA JESSICA ABUBAKAR

ACCOMPLISH PRESS

WWW.ACCOMPLISHPRESS.COM

THE BROKEN HEDGE
Copyright © 2017 Ochuwa Jessica Abubakar

All Rights Reserved. No part of this book may be used, reproduced, stored in or introduced into a retrieval system, or transmitted in any manner whatsoever without written permission from the authors except in the case of brief quotation embodied in critical articles and reviews. Any person who commits any unauthorised act in relation to this publication may be liable to criminal prosecution and civil claims for damages.

Ochuwa Jessica Abubakar has asserted her moral right to be identified as the author of this collection of short stories.

*All characters appearing in this work are fictitious.*
*Any resemblance to real persons, living or dead is purely coincidental.*

Published in the United Kingdom by Accomplish Press
www.accomplishpress.com

Paperback Edition

First published in 2017

Cover Design: RealDreams Media

# Contents

1 THE BROKEN HEDGE ........................................................ 7

2 A PRICE TO PAY ............................................................. 56

3 WAITING ON A WISH ..................................................... 91

4 BRODA AZAYA ............................................................. 166

ABOUT THE AUTHOR ..................................................... 195

A NOTE FROM THE PUBLISHER: ..................................... 197

# ACKNOWLEDGMENTS

I owe all my appreciation to God who blessed me with the gift of writing and for being there for always.

I am grateful to my family-my Mom especially for being there for me all these years, it would have been so much more difficult without your support.

And special thanks to my siblings for the motivation, I would not be here today if not for you.

With love to my beautiful Aunt Anietie Isang. You have inspired me in so many ways that I cannot express here. Thank you so much, Mommy mi.

Thank you, my amazing kin, Oghenovo Ochuko Emore and Grace Okagbare.

Verdcy Giane (Dynamite), you have been so amazing, thank you.

I greatly wish to thank the following people whose help and support made this book possible:

Olawunmi Tolulope Oyebola, you are the angel of my life. Thank you so much for your kindness.

Yetunde Pereira, thank you for helping me think up names for the book and for all the encouragement, you are awesome.

Oge Anukwu and Rachael Asemota-Ighodaro, the twin sisters! I thank you for your kind support. God bless you greatly.

Nicole A. Twum-Baah, you are amazing, thank you so much for the amazing job you did.

Adeola Opeyemi, thank you so much for the good work.

Thank you, Tolulope Popoola, the greatest publisher in history.

Pere Ikidi, thank you so much for your kindness.

Thank you, Jennifer Chinenye Emelife, you are awesome.

Many thanks to my dear friends, Deacon and Deaconess Chizoba,

Special thanks to my dear Pastor Nat Omoruyi and his beautiful wife, Rosita Omoruyi, the Lord bless you and keep you and favor you always. I love you so much.

And much love to my Facebook family and friends for the love and support, seriously, you guys are my inspiration. I thank you greatly. God bless you all.

# 1
# THE BROKEN HEDGE

### *Dedication*

FOR MY FRUITFUL WIVES: AME, OMO,
BLECYN, IFEOMA, ONOME, LARA (SHEKINAH),
NNENNA, LISA, UFUOMA, TESSY, RACHAEL,
MARIANNE, CHIKA, ESE, ANWULI, PRISCILLA
(ASMAU), PRISCILLA (PEARL TUTU), ZUWA,
TONIA, LILLIAN, MILLICENT, CORDELIA,
CATHY, YETTY...

THANK YOU FOR READING ME,
FOR ENCOURAGING AND SUPPORTING ME
ALL THESE YEARS AND FOR HELPING ME
CHOOSE THE TITLE OF THIS STORY.
I LOVE YOU ALL SO MUCH.

When Marissa and I got married, bliss was the word. At a point, I had wondered what all the fuss about marriage was all about. Marriage seemed like the most beautiful thing in the world to me. After all, what is more beautiful than being with a woman who loves you just the way you want to be loved, a woman who understands your mood and listens to you? Most importantly, I thought marriage was about being with someone who had the same sexual appetite as you had. And my marriage was beautiful until it wasn't anymore.

Exactly two years after our wedding, we had our first baby, Jenny. Jenny took after her mother when it came to her looks, she was the cutest baby I had ever seen. Her arrival ushered in a new era in our marriage. It was like an extended happiness had entered our lives. We had such wonderful times together as a family. Simple things like watching Jenny giggle and coo took our breath away.

And then Marissa and I stopped having sex. Things had slowed between us right before the baby came, but it didn't seem to matter because, of course, there was Jenny whom I was so fond of. And besides, Marissa and I still managed to have sex about three times a week, so that was good. Then came Kenny, our second baby, a boy; and everything changed. Marissa stopped wanting to have sex altogether. She pleaded tiredness or a headache every time I touched her.

At first, I didn't make a case out of it. And then I woke up one morning and realized that I hadn't had sex with my wife in two months. I tried to make her understand that we had a problem, but she wouldn't listen. She said she didn't feel as horny as she used to. Her breasts weren't as bouncy as they used to be and her tummy was not as flat. I assured her that none of those things mattered to me because I loved her, and not her body. I used every line known to man to try and convince her to give in and have sex with me, but she refused. So I left her alone and accepted my sad fate. Life became a drag. I felt so frustrated. I was angry all the time. Little things would set me off. As a result, my friends and colleagues began to avoid me. I was sexually frustrated and I couldn't talk to anyone about it for fear that they might mock me. After all, I had boasted in the past about how great my marriage was, so I kept my mouth shut and lived life as I saw it; believing that I would never have sex again. Then Angelina came into my life, and everything changed...

Angelina was an administrative officer where I worked. She wasn't someone I would describe as beautiful, however, she exuded a certain charm and appeal I hadn't experienced before. She had a long neck that I wanted to kiss and full and pouty lips which she always had coloured in red lipstick. Her long and slender legs found me daydreaming often of having them wrapped around my waist. I wondered what that would feel like. And I didn't just find her so appealing because I was sex-starved, it was about more than that. Angelina knew how to charm and compliment me on my work. She obviously adored me.

Every time we closed a deal, it was as if I had won some special challenge. To her, everything I did was cause for celebration. I finally felt like I mattered to someone. It was so endearing because I felt useless at home. I longed to hold her in my arms and make mad love to her. Interestingly, she dropped hints here and there suggesting that she felt the same way. Being a shy person is the only thing that stopped me from pursuing her. I had no idea how to flirt. That was where Rahim came in.

Rahim was also my colleague at work. He was a playboy who was able to talk to girls very easily. He was the one who told me that Angelina was into me. And because I did not want him to know that I already knew that, I acted shocked. As if, the thought had never crossed my mind. If only minds could be read.

Well, he asked me what I was going to do about it and I said nothing because I was a married man.

He laughed and asked, "So, how's the whole married life thing going really?"

My face told him everything he already suspected. I drew a deep breath, relieved to finally let it all out.

That was my first mistake. At first, I thought he was God-sent. He told me that I didn't have to suffer needlessly in my marriage, that I had options. Coming from his mouth, adultery sounded so attractive; I practically heard angels chorusing, "oh how awesome is adultery" in my head.

Wasting no more time, I decided that it was time to end my forced celibacy and heed to his words. According to Rahim, lots of treats awaited me in the adultery business.

Rahim lectured me on how to be a philanderer. He encouraged me to change my entire wardrobe, hairstyle, and perfume. He even advised me to get a new car. It was as if everything about me had changed overnight. I was a new man and I could feel it in my spirit.

I started to stay away from my wife, Marissa, who didn't even seem to notice. Yet, insisted every day that she loved me. How? How could I have a wife who claimed to love me and yet refused to have sex with me? The questions were endless.

ONE FRIDAY MORNING, stimulated by all the lectures Rahim had given me, in addition to my recent transformation, I set out on my way to work. I already knew what I was going to do when I got there. It was what I had to do if I wanted to feel appreciated, and needed, and wanted again.

I got to the office that day feeling very fidgety. I looked for Rahim everywhere but could not find him. Eventually, he found me at my desk trembling.

"Calm down bro," he said, laughing at me. "You must not mess up our plan. Today is seduction day, and you are ready. Go get her!"

I moved away from him, sheepishly, hoping to catch a glimpse of Angelina. Then I saw her a little distance away from where I was standing. She was bent over the copier, her tight skirt accentuating her round, firm, massive buttocks. I gulped for air. The room suddenly felt hot.

I spun on my heels and dashed back into my office. Rahim laughed and came after me. He found me bent over my desk breathing hard for air. I stood up straight and loosened my tie. It suddenly felt very tight. It was as if someone was strangling me with it, except that there was no one pulling on the ends of it.

I could not understand what was happening to me. I had never felt such raw and sudden sexual emotions before. That and the combination of fear made for a very exciting event in my life. At the same time, I felt danger looming. I wasn't supposed to be feeling this way about any woman other than my wife. Well, not even about Marissa. What I felt for her was warm and tender. But this? This was raw... hot ...unusual. I wanted to bite and tear up stuff, throw tantrums. Just anything to purge me of this strange feeling.

RAHIM STOOD IN the doorway of my office shaking his head at me. A smile straightened his lips, a glint of mischief sparkling in his eyes.

"We'll try again tomorrow if you want," he simply said, and I had a feeling he was disappointed in me.

When Rahim left me alone, I tried to be calm. Maybe I could calm down just enough to get some work done so that I could leave work early. Yes, that would be the plan; close early, ask Angelina out for a drink and then drive straight home.

Day one; checked. I settled down and buried myself in work. At noon, I went out to get some lunch at the office cafeteria and Angelina was there. She ate slowly. Everything about her was sensual; the way she closed her mouth over her spoon, bringing it out slowly, the way she sucked at her straw, even the way she swallowed made me excited. I knew I was in trouble, but I didn't want to get out of it. So I sat somewhere in the corner, ordered my lunch and stole glances at her while she ate hers.

Back at work, I was determined to clear my desk before closing. And I almost succeeded in doing until the director sent me a report that needed immediate attention. Of course, Angelina was the one who brought it to my desk. I seized the opportunity and asked her out for a drink. She said okay. I was ecstatic. I put all my attention for the next few hours into finishing up the report, and before long I was done.

When I looked up eventually, it seemed as if the whole office had cleared out. All except for me and Angelina.

We walked out of the office together and she put her hand in mine.

"I just want to feel safe, Greg," she said, smiling up at me. "You make me feel so safe."

I paused to inhale the feeling of being wanted, needed, powerful.

"I'm glad you feel that way with me, Angelina." And with that out of the way, we walked quietly to the bar which was only a few blocks away from the office. We sat side-by-side in one of the booths and ordered some drinks. And while we waited for the drinks to arrive, we talked about ourselves.

Angelina was enchanting. Everything about her was a turn-on. Her smile, her gestures, the way she talked...everything about her was charming. I felt myself falling for her quicker and quicker as the time passed between conversation and drinks.

By the end of the night, I was convinced that I wanted her. I just knew it; I knew that this was it. I wanted this girl forever.

While she talked, I let my eyes wander over her face; her eyes were enormous and moist, like she had tears in them, she had high cheekbones, and the tip of her nose was pointed. She had round nostrils, full lips, and a lovely long neck.

Before I could stop myself, I had my lips on hers. At first, I felt her surprise. It made her hesitate for just a fraction of a second, and then she responded. We kissed slowly at first and then the intensity grew.

Within a minute, we were kissing so passionately, it was as if we were the only two people in the bar that night. I drank in her essence like I needed it to complete mine. She gave as much as I did, kissing me with as much passion as I did her. It was sweet until her hand grazed my thigh and I felt myself grow harder. I felt ready to explode and so with great effort, I wrenched my mouth from hers.

"I'm very sorry, please," I stuttered.

"It's fine, Greg. I just like you so much," she responded, her eyes staring deep into my soul.

"I'm married, Angelina," I croaked painfully.

"I don't care." She grabbed me close and planted her lips on mine.

"Hmmm," was all I could manage. We sank deeper into the kiss from there.

"Let's go to my place" she whispered into my ears. We had been going at it for quite some time, completely unaware of how much time had passed.

I looked at her for a moment. This was going to happen. My excitement knew no bounds. I quickly settled the bill and grabbed her hand. I think we left the bar skipping in sync that night.

---

ANGELINA DID NOT live too far from the office. That made the trip convenient because had we had to go much further, I probably would have changed my mind. But destiny had a different plan in mind. We were meant to do this, and so we did.

We didn't speak at all during the drive to her place. I kept my eyes focused on the road and my ears tuned to her voice giving me directions. *Go straight past that last house, now take a right. Slow down, we will be making a left right after the blue store coming up.* I drove with a sense of urgency. I could not wait to have her.

And soon, we were at her door; me impatient, her rummaging frantically through her bag. When she eventually pulled out her keys, we both exhaled deeply. Within seconds, the door flew open and she was beckoning me in. I walked into the dark space, Angelina following closely behind me. I heard the door shut and the lock turn, and then her breath was on my neck.

I grabbed her from behind me and brought her before me, reaching for her lips with mine. She kissed me back and began to frantically unbutton my shirt. I tried to stay calm as I stripped her of her clothes.

The only light that illuminated the room was a beam from the outside that pierced through the windows. By now, my eyes had become accustomed to the darkness such that I could make out some shapes in the room. There were a sofa and a love seat in the corner of the room. In the middle, there was a small coffee table.

"Where's the bedroom?" I asked her urgently.

By this time, we were both naked. She wasted no time in leading me through another door and into her bedroom. I started kissing her again, my hands running all over her smooth skin. She felt so good to the touch. I kneaded her breasts and kissed her neck, and I hardened some more when she moaned. At that moment, my eyes searched frantically for her bed. I had never seen a bed that inviting. I led her straight to it. We giggled like school kids as we both fell into the softness of the mattress. We were groping at each other now; touching, fondling, kissing, caressing and nibbling on each other.

It was over before we knew it. It had been almost eight months since I had last had a woman so it was not that surprising. And although it did not seem to last that long, it was still the most incredible and most beautiful sex I had ever experienced. I reached over for Angelina and held her tightly, my whole body was trembling.

"It's okay baby," she said and kissed my neck. I smiled. She ran her hands up and down my back before bringing her mouth to mine and kissing me passionately.

I felt myself stirring again. She pushed at my chest gently, urging me to lie on my back, and when I did, she straddled me. She kissed me where she touched me, whispering sweet nothings in my ear. She told me how good kissing and caressing me felt. She twisted, fondled, nibbled and bit on me. I was going crazy; I had never had it this good.

Then she guided me inside her and began to ride me very slowly. The second time was longer, but the third time lasted much longer. And then the fourth time took over, and then we collapsed out of the bed and onto the floor. We were panting hard. We looked at each other and burst into a fit of enjoyable laughter, the kind that said, "wow, I can't believe we just did all that in one night."

It was definitely a great achievement for me. I knew I would not be able to stop smiling for a very long time. I was a stud now, a very satisfied stud, and it showed.

I had no idea what time it was, so I picked up my watch and squinted.

"Shit," I cursed and jumped to my feet. I felt for my clothes on the floor. It was still dark in the bedroom. We had not bothered to turn on the lights the whole time we were ravishing each other.

Angelina sat upright.

"What's the problem, baby?" she asked.

She turned on the bedside lamp and for the first time, I saw what her bedroom really looked like; except that I was too busy looking for my clothes to pay any attention. But when I turned to look at her, I caught my breath. Darkness did her no good. Her hair was everywhere, her eyes were dazed and her lips were swollen. She had the breasts of a Greek goddess, her slim waist led to flared hips. It took all I had to tear my eyes away from her stunning beauty.

"Err..., the time. It's two-thirty," I stuttered. "Where are my clothes? I can't find my clothes!"

"Your clothes are in the sitting room, remember? That's where we got undressed?" she was smiling.

I shook off the memory and headed to the sitting room. Angelina followed.

She helped me get dressed and made sure that I looked neat, with nothing out of place.

"Ok, time to go. I'll miss you though," she said, heading towards the door and holding it open.

"I'll miss you more," I held her briefly at the door and then turned to leave.

"Just a minute," she said. She walked to the bedroom and came out a few seconds later wearing a kimono. I could see that she had nothing on underneath the dress.

She stepped outside with me but I stopped her.

"Why, what's wrong?" she asked.

"Please, you don't have to see me off."

"Why?" she looked puzzled.

"Because ... You look sexy. I don't want anyone else to see you in it.

If Angelina thought my answer was ridiculous given that it was almost three in the morning, she did not say so. Instead, she giggled.

I smiled back at her and bent my head to kiss her before getting in my car and driving out of her compound.

Somewhere between Angelina's house and mine, reality began to dawn on me. I had just committed adultery! Good Lord!

I looked at my appearance in the rear view mirror and smiled. And then I started to feel terrible. I was definitely going to hell.

I fetched my phone from the glove compartment and checked my messages. There were twelve missed calls, but none of them were from Marissa.

"What the hell?!" I had never stayed out this late before, and the one time that I did, my wife couldn't bother to call and check on me? I must admit that Marissa's lack of concern stung me.

I was still brooding over the matter when I received a text message from Angelina. She wanted to know if I had arrived at home. Her text message flooded me with such strong emotions; I called her back immediately. It was nice to feel cared for, to know that someone somewhere cared about whether I had arrived home or not. Even if such person was not the one I was married to.

At the sound of Angelina's voice, all the anger I felt for Marissa dissipated. Angelina had this soft, reassuring voice that made me feel better. We talked until I was almost home. We talked about our night's sexual rendezvous. She made me smile. She asked me to send her a text message once I arrived since a phone call might not be convenient. This girl was simply amazing. I smiled just thinking about how amazing she was.

A few minutes later, I arrived home and drove into the

compound. Marissa was sleeping calmly and didn't even stir when I opened the door. I looked at her with distaste as she slept on, wondering how she could sleep so soundly when her husband hadn't gotten home and it was almost four in the morning. I had not called, and neither had she. Anything could have happened to me out there and she would not even have known.

I shook my head and walked into the bathroom where I soaped my body and reminisced with sweet delight. Then I headed downstairs to find something to eat before getting into bed. I was so relaxed; more than I had felt in a very long time. The thought of Angelina flooded my mind as I lay there with a smiled plastered on my lips. I remembered every detail, every move, every kiss, and every gesture, and I sincerely believed that God was finally rewarding me for all my suffering over the past eight months. That was the only logical explanation I could find to explain this new happiness that was Angelina and me.

I was going to continue seeing her, I just had to. I had found a way to be happy and I was finally going to let go of my misery and embrace my newfound joy and peace. Her name was in my heart as I drifted off to sleep.

---

THAT WAS THE beginning of my affair with Angelina. After closing each day, we went to her place and had sex. At first, we did it like rabbits, as is usually the case at the beginning of relationships. Sex and talk, and sex and talk. We couldn't keep our hands off of each other. I began to spend less time at home. Marissa didn't seem to mind. Even my kids, who had been my consolation when things were really bad between us, began to see less of me. I didn't care anymore.

I spent all my time with Angelina, shopping, movies, quiet bars, and lounges. I loved football, she didn't, but she read up on the club that I supported because she said she wanted to be interested in the things I loved. So every time my team played, we watched it at her place with a big bowl of popcorn and very cold beer. In no time she knew and involved herself in all my likes and encouraged me to be involved in hers too. So we watched football, played chess - which I sucked at by the way - scrabble, tennis, swimming, drinking and sex. Sex, sex, sex!

Interestingly, she never talked down on Marissa. Whenever I expressed anger at Marissa's behaviour, she pleaded with me to be patient with her. She was perfect; every man's dream wife, and I found myself wishing that I had met her before I married Marissa. And the way she made me go home every night, no matter how late it was. Such a thoughtful lady; I often thought.

So we went on with our torrid affair. At first we hid it from our colleagues at the office, but later on, we let it out in the open. Angelina got a lot of criticism from her female colleagues but she didn't care. She said that as long as she made me happy, she was fulfilled. She pampered me openly, massaged me when we got home, bathed me, brushed my hair, she even brushed my eyebrows, cooked all kinds of meals for me and my favourite dishes which she learned and prepared in amazing ways. With her, I was in heaven; worry-free and satisfied.

Rahim wasn't pleased that I was so committed to the affair. He told me many times to slow down with Angelina and try other girls, but I refused. I even reported him to Angelina who only laughed and asked me not to get angry over it because Rahim didn't understand what we had. I calmed down immediately. She was my chill pill.

My affair with Angelina was about 14 months old when I began to notice some changes in Marissa. I got home early one Friday evening because Angelina had gone to visit her parents for the weekend. I was getting ready to turn the key in the front door lock when the door flew wide open to reveal Marissa. She stood there with a smile on her face.

"Hello, honey. Welcome," she said and gave me a hug. I hugged her back and she raised her face to give me a light kiss on my lips. I noticed that she looked different. She had a new hairdo and was wearing makeup. She had on a nice top and shorts. To crown it off, she smelled like flowers. I hadn't really looked at her in a long time and what I saw was pleasing to my eyes. She looked like the old Marissa again, she had even lost the baby fat she gained during her pregnancy.

"Honey, I made dinner," she said, taking my hand awkwardly. "Why don't you go shower while I set the table?"

"Oh, okay" I muttered and dashed upstairs.

In the bedroom, I started pacing. What did this mean? What if the old Marissa came back fully, with sex and all of what we had once had? What would I do? Could I handle having two women at the same time or would I have to let one of them go? Which one would I let go? Could I give them equal attention? I immediately became sad and scared. The questions weighed me down. I needed to talk to someone. Rahim! Yes, I would talk to Rahim. He would know what to do. With that thought came relief and I showered and went back downstairs with dread.

Marissa had made one of my favourite meals; yam pottage with diced chicken sauce on the side. It tasted very good and I didn't leave any of it on the plate. She tried to start a conversation during dinner, but she seemed uneasy, maybe even guilty. I wondered what was going on.

After dinner, I helped her clear up the table and we did the dishes together, this time, silently. After cleaning up, I locked up and we went upstairs. I told her I wanted to check on the kids, something I hadn't done in a long time and I knew it was in a bid to avoid her. I went into the children's room and sat in one of the chairs.

I sat there in the children's room for a long time. When I finally got up to go and face Marissa, I was shaking so badly. But I knew that I couldn't run away from her forever. I entered the bedroom, went into the toilet to take a leak and I got into bed.

We both laid there quietly; neither one of us talked, neither one of us was asleep. I knew from her breathing that she was awake. I was tensed. I knew I wasn't going to sleep anytime soon and I couldn't remain that way either. I thought of going downstairs to watch the TV, but before I could get off the bed, I felt something tender on my arm. I turned to meet Marissa's pleading eyes and her hand on mine. She rubbed and ran her fingers up and down my arm, then slid them to my chest. She moved closer and held me tight. I reached out and touched her arm too. I couldn't reject her. She was my wife and even though she'd rejected my advances a thousand times, I just couldn't bring myself to reject her.

In the darkness, I searched for her lips with mine. She found mine before I did and kissed me. I kissed her back. She moved closer and held me tight. She was shaking and I started to worry.

"Mi…, what's wrong?" I asked, my mouth still on hers.

"Nothing," she replied and kissed me again. She caressed me in an uneven way, which made me realize she was trying too hard. Maybe she'd finally understood she was losing me and wanted to make things right. But of what good will that be to me, I asked myself. I was already in love with someone else.

She touched my ear and I returned back to her. She still knew what I liked and she was doing them all. I decided to let go and started touching her in all the places she loved as well. I just closed my eyes and caressed her. It was easy because I remembered. After a while, it became familiar and I really sunk into it, introducing some stuff I'd never done to her before.

We made love that night, my wife and I; after twenty-two months without sex, we made love, and it was sweet and tender and oh so familiar. It was a bittersweet feeling for me because I loved it and also felt bad because of Angelina.

I heard a sniff from Marissa and I turned to ask what was wrong.

"Nothing, I'm just happy," she answered, but I didn't believe her. I held her close to my side and caressed her hair.

"It's okay, honey. Just go to sleep," I soothed her and she soon fell asleep, snoring softly.

I was in a fix and I knew it. It was a bitch to be found caught in between two women. I tried to gauge my feelings for Marissa; did I still love her or was I just obligated to sleep with her because she was my wife? What was it that caused me to be aroused by her tonight? Love, or because she had looked really sexy? Was I just a stupid sex freak? I had too many questions on my mind with no answers to them. I decided to give myself a break and just sleep. Which I did.

I woke up the next morning to find myself alone in bed. I got up, put on some clothes and went downstairs to find Marissa and the kids. They were watching cartoons; Marissa was in the kitchen. My son, Kenny, saw me and squealed in delight. He ran to me and grabbed my legs, giggling excitedly. I laughed and picked him up and threw him over my shoulder. He was so handsome, he looked just like me. I hoped he wouldn't turn out to be a pig like me too.

Our daughter Jenny muttered a curt "good morning daddy" and continued watching the television. I knew what that meant; trouble. I had to pet, placate and promise her stuff before she loosened up and started chatting with me.

We all ate breakfast together that morning and it was just like old times. It felt good, but I also missed Angelina terribly. I wondered how she was doing. I watched Marissa's movements as she served us, wiped spilled water and milk, and gave one or two orders to the kids. It really felt good to be home again.

After breakfast, I played with the kids for some time and then went upstairs to shower and get ready for my outing. Normally, I did not inform Marissa of my whereabouts, but after what had happened last night, I felt I owed it to her. So told her that I was seeing a colleague at work.

I left the house and drove straight to Rahim's place.

As soon as I got to his place, he came out, got into my car and we drove off. We did not want his wife to be in on our discussion, so we had to take this as far away from his house, and mine, as possible. The thought of Rahim being married always gave me pause. He was married to a timid girl who never spoke in public, except to say hello.

Anyway, we drove to a bar and ordered drinks, and then I spilled my guts.

"Wait, wait, you mean Marissa finally agreed to have sex with you?" he looked shocked and somewhat pissed.

"Not just agreed, she made me agree too. She came on to me Rahim, and I just couldn't say no. She's still my wife you know…"

"Yeah, right. A wife who has paid you zilch attention in ages," he hissed. He looked really offended and I was a little uneasy about his strong reaction. I mean, I knew he had my best interest at heart but Marissa was still my wife. Maybe I had upset something in his player code, I wasn't sure.

"Rahim, all I want to know is what to do. Can you please tell me what to do?"

Rahim looked at me in a scolding way and shook his head.

"You're in love with Angelina, right?"

I nodded.

"Do you think you can let her go?" he asked.

"I don't know if I have it in me to do that. I love her too much," I said sadly.

"And Marissa?" he asked, tilting his head to one side.

"She's my wife, the mother of my kids. I kind of have to love her, I must love her right?"

"No, you don't! She's been anything but fair to you. She's just trying to mess with your mind. She's probably found out about your affair with Angelina, that's why she's being all nice now. She just wants to eat her cake and have it too. She forced you into this. You have to stand as a man and do what you have to do."

"And what's that?" I held my breath.

"Get a divorce and be free, man. Be free to love whomever you choose to love." He looked exasperated.

"For real? Wow! I don't know Rahim. It sounds so final. What will happen to my kids?" I must admit that the idea of divorcing Marissa had crossed my mind a couple of times. It was something I had played with in my mind but I had never thought about it too deeply. I sighed audibly and got up.

"Well, I better go because there isn't much to talk about here. I pretty much have my options laid out before me. It's left for me to choose one," I said to Rahim resignedly.

"That's right buddy. I'm sure you'll make the right choice." Rahim patted me on my back.

"Yeah," I nodded. Then Rahim signalled to the waiter to settle the bill.

I reached into my pocket and pulled out my phone. Angelina answered on the first ring and we talked for some time before ending the call. Her voice was gay and soft. She said she was having a good time with her folks. It made me happy to hear that she was having a good time. I dropped Rahim off at his house and drove home. The drive home was one that I dreaded. I wasn't really interested in facing Marissa just yet. I wondered if she'd want to have sex again.

Damn! If we continued having sex, things could get complicated. But how was I going to be able to deny her what she was entitled to? According to the Bible, she owned my body, and I'd shamelessly given it to someone else who had no right to it. But then again, how could I quote the Bible when I hadn't been to church in a long time? How could I possibly sit through a sermon, knowing that I wasn't living right? My mind drifted to Angelina again and I found relief. I could go to her place; she had given me a key. I could hide out there and not have to go home just yet.

And that's exactly what I did. I drove to her place, let myself in, and went straight to the bed and got into it. Her sweet smell that clung to the sheets wafted into my nostrils. I definitely wasn't going to be thinking anything sensible in this bed so I just let myself relax, enjoying the peace and quiet. Apart from the occasional sound of a car driving by, it was really peaceful.

I must have dozed off, because when I woke up, it was dark outside. I got up from the bed and went into Angelina's mini kitchen to get some cold water from the fridge. My throat felt dry so I just drank straight from the bottle. Then I went to the parlour, turned on the television and sat down to watch. I knew I was stalling but I also knew at some point I would have to go home to Marissa. I didn't know whether to be happy or sad. I just needed to make a decision very fast. I had to talk to Angelina about this. It was a good thing she was coming back into town the following day.

Finally, I got up and left for home. Again, Marissa was at the door to welcome me. But she did not kiss me this time. Was this going to be a routine? Was she really messing with me as Rahim believed? Was she? I didn't feel safe anymore because she hadn't even said anything about the past year. Was she thinking we would just continue as if nothing had happened? It was hard to stomach, too hard.

We ate dinner in silence. Afterwards, I went upstairs to bed. The kids were already asleep so there was no excuse to linger in their room. I laid on my side of the bed and turned my back to her like I had done the night before. She did not seem like she wanted to make a move and I was fine with that. Or maybe I wasn't. Had I become unattractive to her again? My mind was still racing when I heard her call my name.

"Yes?" I answered gruffly.

"Do you want to have sex again?" her tone was tentative. I didn't answer her right away because I didn't know the answer to her question. Did I or did I not? I remembered how the previous night had gone and I knew that I wanted her again. It wasn't hot and feverish like it was with Angelina but I wanted to repeat what we'd done yesterday.

"Well, do you?" I asked her, bending backwards to see her expression.

"Yes," she said quickly.

"Okay," I said and I turned fully to face her. We kissed slowly and softly. I didn't understand how I could still want her so much, especially since I had believed that that part was over. But here I was enjoying her warmth and savouring the taste of her lips. I pulled her tight to close the small distance between us and kissed her deeply. We made love slowly and surely, we did it twice and it was so good. I took the lead in everything. I was in charge and it felt good, a feeling I had not felt for a long time, especially since Angelina was always in charge. I felt like a stud with Angelina, but with Marissa, I felt like a man. It was a nice feeling, very familiar; like I was finally home. I always knew there was something missing in my affair with Angelina. This was what had been missing. This was it.

Marissa was my essence. I felt complete with her. No doubt that I'd enjoyed the sexual adventure with Angelina. I enjoyed the rawness of it, but that truth was that that kind of thing had never really appealed to me. I was the domesticated kind, homely. The kind of man some people referred to as goody-two-shoes.

Later that night, I stared at Marissa while she slept. I knew I was going to go with her. She was obviously back and willing to make our marriage work. I would not divorce her. I loved her still.

I had never stopped loving her, even though I had stopped seeing her. What I felt for her hadn't diminished one bit. It was all back. I closed my eyes and drifted off to sleep, only to be awakened later to soft moaning. I listened in the night, realizing that the sound was coming from Marissa. She was probably dreaming. I started to wake her up and stopped. I couldn't make out what she had said and so I leaned a little closer. She said it again and I felt the hairs on my body stand up. Then she said it again and I became as still as a corpse.

"Rahim," she whispered again and I felt my ears explode.

"What the hell?" I yelled jumping out the bed, waking Marissa up with a start, a bewildered look on her face.

"What is it?" she asked, scrambling out of bed, looking scared.

I stared at her in disbelief, shaking uncontrollably. Words failed me.

"Honey, what is it?" she asked, coming towards me.

"Don't!" I almost screamed. "Don't you come one step closer to me," I said, quietly this time.

"Greg, you're scaring me. What happened?" she looked worried and reached out to touch me.

"Don't touch me!" I yelled. "I said don't touch me!"

"Would you please tell me what's going on?" she yelled back.

"Rahim?" I said through gritted teeth. She gasped. And then she began to shiver. She shook so badly that I began to worry that something could be wrong with her. But then I remembered why she was shaking and worry turned back into anger.

"Marissa, please explain to me right now why you were calling another man's name in your sleep. And it better be another Rahim, not my friend," I warned.

Marissa started to sob and I knew it was him. That bastard!

"So it's him?" I asked. She nodded between sobs.

"Look at me!" I commanded her. She raised her tear-filled eyes and looked at me.

"You were calling Rahim, my friend?" I could not believe this was happening.

"Yes," she cried.

I braced myself before I asked the next question.

"Did you sleep with him?"

"No, I did not."

She started to move towards me and I shook my head and pointed to where she'd been standing. Okay, she hadn't slept with him. I had to ask the next question.

"Did he touch you?" she didn't answer. She just sobbed some more.

"I said did he touch you?"

My eyes were like coals of fire.

"Yes, he did." she was crying hard now.

"He touched you," I said almost to myself and fell onto the bed.

"Greg, please don't do this. I'm sorry, let's talk about it, please." She came and knelt before me, holding on to my legs and sobbing badly. I felt numb; like I wasn't there.

"What do you want us to talk about? About how you slept with another man?" I asked smiling wryly. I was smiling in the midst of tragedy.

"I didn't sleep with him, I just kissed him," she said.

"What? That's even worse! Because when you kiss, you feel stuff. That's why prostitutes don't kiss!" I yelled and burst out crying.

We both sat there crying. I was finished. That bastard Rahim had kissed and touched my wife, all the while pretending that he was my friend. No wonder he had been so angry when I told him that Marissa and I had made love. Was that jealousy? Was he in love with my wife? I needed to know everything that had happened between them before divorcing Marissa because I sure was going to do that now. Painfully, there was no relief in it.

"Greg, honey, please let's talk about this, please," she continued to plead.

"You know what? I don't want to hear anything from you. You cheated on me!" I cried.

"And what about you? You think I don't know about your escapades with that slut Angelina?" she shouted angrily.

"I'm a man Marissa, I'm allowed to cheat but you are not, especially not with my friend. Yes, I had an affair and newsflash lady, it was all your fault!"

"How?" she looked confused.

"I'll tell you how. You starved me of your body. You didn't allow me to touch you. You withheld sex from me for eight good months, Marissa. Yes, I counted. What was I supposed to do? I'm a man. I need sex like I need air. Without sex, I am nothing. You turned me into nothing and that "slut" brought me back." I was yelling, my heart pounding fiercely.

"Oh God!" She cried with her face in her hands.

"Marissa, whatever possessed you to get involved with Rahim?" I finally asked her.

"He was nice to me," she said. "He was kind, caring, and sympathetic. I wouldn't have gone so far with him if I had known you weren't going to leave me. He said you were going to. I thought our marriage was dead," she said quietly.

"Well, you sure had a hell of a time at the wake," I said with heavy sarcasm.

"Please, don't say that, please," she pleaded.

"You are going to tell me everything that happened, otherwise I'm going to bring this house down tonight," I threatened.

"I will, I will, please don't," she agreed quickly. Then she started talking.

"Greg, you know that I love you, I've always loved you, and I always will. Marrying you was the most wonderful thing that has ever happened to me because you're the best man alive. Remember the fun we had during our courtship? It was amazing and we both knew we were meant to be together." She paused and then continued.

"Everything was wonderful and even better when Jenny came. We were the happiest couple around and we were envied by others."

Tears started falling from her eyes.

"But when Kenny came, something happened to me. You remember I had a big tear from my cervix down to my vagina during delivery because he was a really big baby? That wound did something to me. I became afraid of having anything go inside of me, even after the wound had healed and the stitches had come off."

"Shit!" I exclaimed.

"Don't, please let me finish. I didn't prevent you from making love to me because I was wicked or because you weren't attractive to me anymore, or because I didn't love you anymore. I did not have sex with you because I was afraid, Greg."

"You should have said something," I retorted.

"Yes, I should have but I just felt I would overcome it. But then months went by and I didn't. I was overwhelmed. You always wanted to have sex, you always made the first move. At first, I felt that was how it was supposed to be, but then I read somewhere that women should initiate sex as well. But you never gave me a chance to. You never made me hunger for you. You were always so into it." She spoke succinctly.

"Well, forgive me for wanting to make love with my wife all the time." I knew it was a cheap shot, but I felt defensive because she was right.

"So I denied you sex for a very long time, which eventually led you into the arms of another woman. I knew when it all started because you went completely out of character. Even though we weren't having sex, I'd caught you severally, staring at me, giving me the look which I'm ashamed to say, I always ignored. But you stopped looking at me altogether, you changed your wardrobe, wore a different cologne, and above all, you started coming home late, reeking of perfume and sex.

I tried to stomach it because you didn't give me much opportunity to talk to you as you were always out of the house. I told myself that whatever you were doing with her didn't matter, but after a while, I couldn't take it anymore. Then I decided to talk to my friend, Rosa…"

"Rosa? That crazy woman?" I asked incredulously. Rosa was our neighbour and friend, somewhat. She was indeed crazy. She was always fighting her husband, Dennis. He had voiced his complaints to me on many occasions. I couldn't believe that Marissa talked to Rosa about our problems.

"Yes, Rosa," she continued. "I didn't want to say anything to our family." As if this was a better choice.

"Well, Rosa told me to go and confront you and Angelina at

the office. According to her, if I did that she would be so ashamed that she would leave you alone. I didn't agree right away, but I kept thinking about it. And the more I thought about it, the more sensible it seemed. So one day, I went to your office to do just that…"

"…And that was how you met Rahim," I said, finishing off her sentence.

"Yes." she lowered her eyes.

"Okay. Continue," I said quietly.

"When I got to your office, you weren't there. Neither was she. Rahim said you had gone for lunch and that he didn't know where. I wanted to wait for you to return, but he said there was no point. He asked me how I had come and I told him that I had come in a cab. So he offered to take me home. I accepted his offer because I was tired. On the drive home, I asked him if he knew about your affair, he said he did not. And that's when he promised me that he would help me find out what was going on. Then he asked me why I was concerned, that I was your wife and that even if you had anything with anyone else, I would always be your wife. And I told him that it didn't feel so simple to me anymore. I opened up and told him everything. I don't know why, but I did. He was really sympathetic. He seemed to feel terrible about it and that made me feel relaxed with him. He said I had done nothing to warrant being cheated on and that I shouldn't beat myself up about it. He told me how beautiful I was and that if you didn't appreciate me, then you were a loser."

She said the last word in a hushed tone before she continued.

"He dropped me at home and asked for my number so that he could reach me when he had any information about you and

Angelina. I gave it to him and went inside. That was how it all began. He called me every time, just to talk. He was attentive and nice. At first, we talked over the phone; then he started coming over to the house during lunch break. He told me all that he knew about your affair with Angelina. He even took me to her place one day. He told me you were too committed to Angelina to remain in our marriage and I began to believe that. Then one day, he kissed me…"

"Damn!" I stood up from the bed and went to the window.

"Please, Greg, let me finish, please."

"Go on," I said.

"At first I resisted, but then he asked me why I was holding back, that as he was speaking, you were with Angelina enjoying yourself and I was choosing to suffer. He tried to kiss me again and this time I let him. I'm so sorry, honey. I let him kiss me. I even kissed him back. He didn't try to go further than that, he just kissed me. It became our thing, he would come over during his break and we would kiss. He told me to begin to pay attention to myself; make my hair, wear stylish clothes, smell good and just be happy. And I obeyed him completely. I threw out my maternity and nursing clothes and bought some new stuff. I registered at a fitness club so I could shed my excess weight. I even began to apply for jobs wherever I heard of vacancies. I did so many new things. Rahim said he was proud of me. He said things that lifted my spirit, he encouraged me to do new things and applauded my every accomplishment. Greg, that was hard, so hard to resist, especially as I wasn't getting anything from you. So I let myself go and his advances grew bolder. I never thought of having sex with him and he never asked for it. Well, at first, he didn't. He just kissed me, and subsequently...." She paused, looking at me with so much remorse in her eyes.

"Subsequently what?" I asked through gritted teeth.

"He touched me," she said quietly.

"How far did he go?" I asked, a large lump in my throat.

She started crying again and I got up angrily. "Marissa, your tears don't move me. Tell me what I want to know"

"Everything, Greg. Everything apart from sex!" she cried.

"Did you enjoy it?" I asked. My fists were clenched.

"Greg, please," she pleaded.

"Answer me, dammit. Did you enjoy it?" I yelled.

She didn't answer me. She just kept sobbing.

"Oh my God, you enjoyed it, didn't you? I grabbed her by the arms and began to shake her. She just kept on crying and I pushed her onto the bed, crumbled on the floor and started crying. Broken to my core. I felt old and drained. I felt terrible and I doubted if I would ever survive it. We just stayed there crying.

After some time we both quietened down, both of us lost in our own thoughts. I felt I was done. How could she have done this to me? How? I felt terrible, uncomforted. To think that she had known all along what I had been doing with Angelina. And the stuff I did with her was far more than what she'd done with Rahim. That sobered me up because if she'd felt half of what I was feeling now then it must have been horrible for her. Then and only then did I understand that cheating from either partner had the same emotional effect on each of them. The fact that I was a man and that it was widely acceptable for a man to cheat didn't make it less painful for a woman. And emotional pain is the worst of all pain ever. I felt light, like paper and it wasn't a good feeling.

"Marissa, how did you feel when you heard about my affair?" I asked quietly.

"I died," she answered softly and I closed my eyes tightly.

"Yeah," I smiled sadly. "So, what happened next?" I asked and she sighed. "Please, Marissa, I really want to know."

"Okay. Well, like I said, he got bolder and then one day he tried to have sex with me, but I refused. He got angry and started calling me names. He said I was a tease and he was sick of me. He got really angry and said after all he'd done for me, I still didn't want to have sex and that I was going to die with my secondary virginity, and so many other horrible things. That day, I saw him for what he really was and told him to get out of my life and to never come back. I was shaken by his words and wondered if perhaps he was right.

"So, I decided that I was going to change. I sought for help from books and the internet. But mostly, I just prayed asking God for forgiveness and restoration of my sexuality and then my marriage. After some time, I felt peace in my heart, and that was when I started being nice to you again, initiating sex with you and all that. I never knew that you would accept me back so quickly and I was so glad when you did. But I was still uncomfortable because of the time I had spent with Rahim and the things we had shared. I told myself that I was going to tell you, but I was scared. So when you heard me call his name..." She drifted off.

We became quiet again, lost in our own thoughts. I wanted to kill Rahim. I was sure that I would. He was such a snake. And to think that I had thought he was being good to me. I thought of how much I'd told him about my escapades with Angelina and I hated him so much. I wanted bad things to happen to him.

"What are we going to do? Marissa asked softly.

"I don't know," I answered. She sighed. We became quiet again. We stayed that way for a long time. After a while, I heard a cock crow and that was when I realized that we had been up all the night.

I picked my phone from the table and looked at the time, it was five-thirty in the morning. I sat the phone back down and went to the window and parted the curtain, first light had appeared.

"Well, we can't sleep now," Marissa said, looking at the light grey clouds that peeked between the parted curtains. "We have to get ready for church."

"Stop it." I could not believe what I was hearing. Was she really talking about going to church after everything we had just let out in the open? No.

"Stop talking as if nothing is wrong because everything is wrong. We cheated on each other, emotionally and physically and it is not normal," I snapped at her.

"You think I don't know that?" She asked.

"Then stop pretending!" I yelled.

"I'm not pretending. I just responded to what you said. Is this how it's going to be around here? Are we going to be at each other's throat all the time? What do you want to do to make things right? Tell me what you want and I'll do it!!!" she screamed.

"I want a divorce!!!" I screamed back at her and she gasped.

"No, no, no," she shook her head. "I don't want a divorce. We can work this out, me and you, please, baby."

She moved close to me and buried her face in my chest, weeping and my heart broke a million times over. I couldn't remember ever making her cry in the time we've been together so it hurt. I couldn't bear it so I held her as she wept and didn't turn away when she raised her face and kissed my lips. I let her kiss me until she whispered, "Rahim is not an issue, baby, please. It's you I will always want, my baby"

I pushed her away and pointed a trembling finger at her, "Don't call me that. And don't you come near me. I don't want you near me anymore, ever. I don't even want to see you!" I stormed out of the room, banging the door loudly behind me.

I went downstairs and flopped down on one of the sofas. Everything was all messed up. I knew I was being a hypocrite, but I just couldn't help it. I couldn't accept the fact that my own wife had allowed another man to touch her. I was being very selfish, this I admitted. I had also allowed another woman to touch me. We were going through the same emotional torture. I understood her when she said she had died when she heard about my infidelity. But what was I supposed to do? Was I supposed to just pat her on her back and continued living with her as though nothing had ever happened? Something had happened, something terrible, and I felt like there was nothing we could do to remedy it.

And it was all my fault. I blamed myself, yes. I should have tried to find out what was wrong with her. I was her husband, her protector. How in the world had I allowed things to slide so badly? What could I do now? Would I ever smile again? I felt sick to my stomach.

I must have dozed off because I woke up to gentle nudging. It was Marissa, she was dressed and ready for church.

"We're ready for church," she said. "Would you like us to wait while you get ready so we can all go together? She asked.

"No, you guys go on, I'm not in the mood." I dismissed her.

From the clock on the wall, it was 9:00 a.m. already. I had slept for about two hours. It only hit me then that Angelina was flying in with the morning flight and I was supposed to pick her up.

"Okay. There's food in the microwave, please eat something," she begged.

"Not hungry, but thanks," I replied.

She looked at me with pleading eyes then turned and walked away, calling out for the kids to come downstairs. I quickly got up and went into the guest room because I didn't want to see them. I wasn't sure I could act normal around them. It would take too much from me and I was already drained. I only came out after I heard Marissa's car pull away from the compound. I went upstairs, took a quick shower, got dressed and rushed out of the house. For the first time, I was not excited to see Angelina. I didn't feel like talking to anyone.

---

I GOT TO the airport about ten minutes before Angelina's flight arrived. I waited for her outside the arrival hall.

"Hey," I said with a dry smile when she was finally in front of me. "How was your trip? Your folks?"

She hugged me.

"Oh, very well thanks," she said.

We walked out to the car hand in hand. On the drive to her place, she seemed to talk nonstop. I was barely listening.

Then she whispered something in my ear. Normally, this kind of talk would have gotten me excited, but this time, it didn't. I'd missed her at first, but after the revelation I had last night, she was the last person I wanted to see.

"You look so serious, baby. What's wrong?"

"Huh? Oh, nothing. I'm just tried." I smiled at her, hoping that she would drop it.

"Hmmm," she said, smiling and wiggling her silicate fingers in the air. "One massage coming right up then."

"Babe, you don't have to, really." I patted her thigh. Big mistake! She grabbed my hand, raised it to her lips and kissed it. Then she traced the inside of my palm with the tip of her tongue. I felt myself stir. What was it about a man's sexual arousal against his reasoning? My head was too unsettled to think about having sex, but my penis was responding to Angelina's every touch.

Maybe one last tumble in the hay with Angelina wasn't such a bad idea. After all, Marissa already knew about her so I wouldn't be committing a new crime. I turned to look at Angelina. She smiled at me through dimmed eyes. Damn, she was sexy. And she knew it. Everything she did worked. All her moves, tricks, they got the job done. I had to applaud her. Silently, though.

She jumped on me the moment we shut the door when we arrived at her place. We kissed. We tore off our clothes. And before long, I was pounding away at her on her sitting room floor. I was angry, and for the first time since we'd gotten together, I took her roughly. She screamed in ecstasy, her face tight with sweet pain.

Then I ejaculated. We were both breathless.

"Oh my goodness! Greg, where did that come from?" She was gasping in between words and I could feel her legs trembling.

I mumbled something, got up, and started to get dressed.

"Where are you going?" She propped herself up on her elbows and looked at me with a puzzled look.

"Home," I said quietly.

"This early? We haven't even started."

"We've done enough for today," I said, trying not to sound so tight.

She continued to stare at me.

"I have to go and take care of some stuff," I said, choosing my words carefully.

"Well, are you coming back?"

"I don't know."

Angelina stood up. My heart raced.

"What's going on, Greg? Talk to me, please. Is it about Marissa?"

"Don't, please. I have to go now. I'll talk to you later." I gave her a peck on the cheek and left her rooted in the same spot, a look of confusion pressed on her face.

"Dammit!" I cursed loudly as I drove away. "Fool!"

I had only driven for a minute or two when my phone rang. I ignored her call and kept driving.

After the fifth ring, she gave up.

I continued driving, but not towards home. I drove to the beach instead. The breeze would help me think. I needed some place quiet to think. And that is exactly what I found. It was quiet when I got there and I was thankful for that. I walked up and down the beach trying to think of how best to put my life back together. I sat on the sand and looked up at the spread of the sky and wished that I could soar with the clouds. I wished I were a baby, free of this huge weight on my shoulders. I wished for a lot of things, but none could happen of their own volition. I had to make a decision and I had to make it fast. There was no way I could continue like this.

First things first; I had to stop cheating. Marissa had stopped, so I had to stop too. No more rendezvous with Angelina. I would return her key to her tomorrow. After that, I had to sort things out with Rahim. I was so ready to punch him hard. He deserved it. He had violated the code. I had to see him and I had to see him immediately.

I left the beach and drove in the direction of Rahim's house. I called to tell him I was coming. He said he was home.

His wife was the one who let me in.

"Hey man," Rahim said, walking towards me with his hand stretched out for a handshake.

I ignored his hand and flew my fist into his face instead. He had not seen that coming. He staggered backward and tried to steady himself. But he couldn't. My punch landed him against one of the sofas.

"Shit!" He looked rightly confused.

I lunged forward and crowded over him, pinning him against the sofa, punching him over and over again while he tried to cover his face with his hands.

"Mr. Greg! Please, stop!" His wife's voice sounded so far away even though she was standing right next to me, trying to pull me off her husband.

"Don't kill him, please!"

I ignored her. My anger had made me deaf and I was blinded by my rage at the way that I had been deceived.

"Please, leave him alone, for the sake of his children, please!"

I'm not sure if it was the word children that made me stop, but I began to sober up. I stopped hitting him and stood up. I was breathing hard.

I looked at him with disgust.

"If I ever see you near my wife again, I'll kill you."

His wife gasped.

"Your wife?" She asked incredulously.

"Shut your trap and get out of here, woman!!!" Rahim yelled at her and she scurried away.

"Rahim, you tried to have sex with my wife. I called you my friend," I said quietly.

"See, Greg, I'm sorry. Please, let's talk about this."

"I have no desire to talk to you, now or ever. Just stay away from me and everything that concerns me, okay?"

I walked out of Rahim's house and drove some distance before I noticed that my hands hurt. It was only then that I wondered what his face and ribs must feel like. The thought of the pain I must have left gave me some satisfaction and I smiled to myself.

The next thing on the agenda was to sever ties with Angelina. I drove back to Angelina's place. When she saw me she smiled pleasantly, thinking I'd come back for another bout of sex. I could see the shock on her face when I told her what I had come for. I dropped her key on the table and walked out.

I began to feel lighter, but there was still the issue of me and Marissa. Our marriage. Forward or never again? I knew it was up to me to decide that, but I was torn.

I got home around 6:00 p.m. and was greeted by a delicious aroma that caused my stomach to rumble. I hadn't eaten all day. I hadn't even noticed. I walked into the kitchen. Luckily, there was no one there. My mouth watered at the sight of the food; fried rice, coleslaw, and roasted chicken. I could not wait to dig in.

*"Easy there,"* I said to my stomach as I heaped some rice onto my plate. I added two portions of coleslaw and a large drumstick and took a big bottle of coke from the fridge. Then I at the table

ready to devour the meal before me. The first bite tasted heavenly. Marissa could cook. That was one of her qualities; I just had to hand it to her. Everything she made was delicious. With Angelina, it was different. We spent more time eating out than at her place, which was why I still ate at home during the affair. Even the few times when she managed to cook, she still couldn't hold a candle to Marissa in that area.

I wolfed down everything; the food, drink, and water. Afterwards, I washed the plate, went back to the living room, and sat down to watch some TV.

I was watching the news when Marissa came in. She'd been asleep. I could tell from the look of her hair. It was tousled, her eyes looked dreamy and her lips soft. She was beautiful.

"Hi," she said softly.

"Hi," I answered.

"Have you eaten?" She asked.

"Yeah," I answered.

"Okay." She sounded relieved. Maybe she had thought that I was going to stop eating her food. If I did, it still wouldn't solve anything. Besides, her food was just too tasty to pass up so I would just have to keep eating it.

"Where are the kids?" I asked her.

"In their room, doing their homework," she replied.

"Okay, I'll go and check on them in a while."

Marissa came and sat down beside me and we watched the TV together. She understood my mood so she didn't try to talk about our situation or touch me. She just sat there, quietly. I felt a sense of comfort so much so that after a while I relaxed and drifted off to sleep. She must have straightened me out on the sofa because when I woke up two hours later, I was lying fully stretched. I stood up and stretched, yawning loudly. It was past nine so I locked up the house and went upstairs. On the way to our bedroom, I looked in on Jenny and Kenny. They were already asleep, so I kissed them both and left.

Marissa was reading the Bible in bed. I got my stuff ready for work the next day, took a shower and went downstairs to the guest room to sleep. I didn't want to make love to her anymore, I needed time to myself. I needed to think right.

So after that night, I took to sleeping in the guest room. At first I did not lock the door, but after Marissa came in once, begging me to return upstairs on the first night, I never forgot to lock the door. She had said things would worsen if we slept apart, but I didn't care. I needed all the time I could get, alone.

The kids had no idea what was going on because they were just as happy as they'd always been. Plus, they were seeing more of me.

Life went on and I took each day as it came, believing that something would happen that would help me decide on what to do. At home, I played with the kids, made small talk with Marissa; helped her out whenever she needed me to and so on. We still weren't having sex, but she knew I wasn't cheating anymore. At the office, I concentrated on my job, meeting deadlines and closing deals. I was more serious about my job than I'd been before.

Meanwhile, Angelina couldn't believe that I had left her, that I could leave her. She had thought that I was too hung up on her and that nothing could tear us apart. In all truthfulness, it had been that way at a point. However, I have always been a very principled man. That never went away even though it was buried deep when Angelina came along. When push came to shove, however, I knew how to do the right thing.

So she avoided me. Rahim too. He never came near my office. Since the last incident, I'd seen him just once; in the canteen, he'd taken off as soon as he saw me. My life was almost back to normal. What was still missing was my emotional and sexual relationship with my wife. I still loved her, of that I was sure. I just didn't feel it. I knew I wanted to make love to her but I held myself in check. I tried to make as little contact with her as possible because I wasn't sure that I would be able to resist her if I did touch her. And so we continued living as husband and wife, barely speaking, but each of us carrying out our respective duties.

One day, after constantly battling and struggling with myself, I decided to attend midweek service. I knew that I needed direction. I'd read books and surfed the internet for weeks, but the hole in my heart was still there, so I decided that perhaps a sermon was what I needed.

The service ended up being just what I had needed. I enjoyed every bit of the message and I was really glad I went. After service, I was heading out of church when I felt a hand on my arm. I turned and saw that it was the Pastor.

"Good evening, Pastor," I greeted him respectfully.

"Good evening, Greg. How have you been?" he smiled.

"Good sir," I answered, smiling back at him.

"Are you in a hurry? I'd like us to talk," he said to me.

"Of course, sir, I'm not rushing anywhere," I admitted.

"Good. Then let's go to my office."

I followed him as he led the way to his office a few yards away.

"Please, sit." He offered me a chair once we had entered. The room was warm and welcoming. Its aura provided comfort. It felt peaceful in there and I wanted to remain there forever because that was the kind of atmosphere I yearned for.

"So, Greg, tell me. What's going on with you?" He said, smiling and settling into his chair.

"Nothing much, sir. Work, family, you know…"

"Hmmm. You've been missing from church for months now," he said, looking directly at me.

"Yes, sir. I've been busy."

"Okay, okay, I see." He was still smiling. "So how have you been coping without hearing the word for months now?"

I wanted to say "fine" but I knew I'd be lying. It wasn't fine at all. It had been bad.

"Not too good," I admitted, looking down. "So many things have gone wrong."

"I thought so," he mused. "Would you like to tell me about it?"

I sighed audibly, and then nodded.

"Okay. Please, go on," he spoke with such kindness that before I knew it, I was spilling everything to him. I told him about how Marissa denied me sex, told him about Angelina, Rahim and about everything that had happened.

He nodded along, not interrupting me once, no expression of judgment on his face. He seemed interested, understanding, and he even looked like he felt bad for me. I felt so relieved that I'd finally been able to talk about my problems and not feel guilty at all.

After I stopped talking, he was quiet for a while. And then he asked me, "What do you intend to do now, son?"

"I don't know, sir. I'm sure I still love my wife, but I just can't get past the fact that another man has touched her the way that I have."

"I understand," he nodded. "But you do know that another woman has touched you the way that your wife has too, right?"

"Yes, I know that. I just feel that it's different because I'm a man and she's a woman."

"It's not, son. Your wife feels more broken than you do, the difference is that women have more of a capacity to forgive than men do," he explained.

I was quiet.

"Do you know what happened here?" He asked. I shook my head indicating that I did not.

"Ecclesiastes 10:8. That's what has happened. The hedge around your marriage was broken and the serpent bit. Marissa came to me some time ago and told me what was going on. I explained it to her this way: that she had broken the hedge around your marriage by not meeting your sexual needs and that was why you went out. Let me tell you what a hedge is." He paused and leafed through a journal on his desk absent-mindedly. "A hedge is a close set of bushes lined up in a straight row. It forms a fence in a garden as a means of protection against something. Christians must remain attentive to avoid being bitten by the serpent. The poison that is injected into the body is deadly if left untreated. Our spiritual hedge can be broken through lack of communion with God, unforgiveness, holding grudges, not reading and meditating on the word of God, and being carnally minded. When this happens, we become easy prey for the enemy. You also should have done your best to find out what the problem was from your wife. You should have come to me and we would have handled it together."

By this time, my shoulders were shaking as I sobbed.

The pastor continued. "But don't despair, for there's absolutely nothing that God cannot restore."

"Pastor, I don't know what to do now," I cried.

"Return to God. Make up for time lost by spending time with Him again, renew your relationship with Him and everything else will fall into place."

"But I feel…"

"Stop feeling so much, Greg. Walk by faith, not by what you feel. I know you don't feel like having sex with your wife. Well no one is forcing you to. After all, you have the rest of your lives to do that. Just focus on God for now. You obviously feel bad about what you did, so first things first; forgive yourself. Then forgive your wife. Then forgive the other parties involved. Try talking with Marissa again, not just about the kids, find out things from her. Communicate with her. Ask her what she wants to do with her life now because I believe it'll be different from when you two just got married. Whatever she wants to do, support her in it, help her grow, spend time with your kids, take the spiritual lead in your home, and, my son, you will live to enjoy the proceeds until it is time for you to join the Lord."

"Yes sir. Thank you so much, sir." I was grateful.

"You're welcome, son. Let's pray." The pastor stood up and I knelt before him. He placed his right hand on top of my head and prayed. "Father, I present your son to you this day asking that you forgive him and heal his home. Look past all that he has done and have mercy on him and his family. Protect them from the works of the evil one and preserve their lives. Help them to hunger and thirst after you all the time. Restore all that has been lost and give them your peace which surpasses all understanding in Jesus's name. Amen."

"Amen," I echoed and stood up. "Thank you, Pastor, I'm very grateful" I almost hugged him.

"Thank you for coming to church today. See you on Sunday," he said as he walked me to the door.

"Most definitely, sir," I said profusely, stepping out of the office.

"God bless you," he said, waving goodbye.

---

THE MEETING I had with the Pastor that day changed me. I decided that I did not want a divorce anymore. I still didn't want to have sex with Marissa, but I began to pay more attention to her. I even started to smile at her, sometimes telling jokes and teasing her. I invested in a business she wanted to pursue and I helped her build it by taking care of the financial aspect, using my experience as an accountant.

At work, my disposition improved. I greeted my colleagues effusively and tried not to frown when I saw Rahim.

One day, I called Angelina into my office and apologized to her. I explained to her that I was sorry to have wasted her time and given her false hope. To my surprise, she laughed and said I had never given her false hope because I had never promised her anything. She said she had understood what she was doing all along; she knew I was married and there was no future in it for her. She said she just felt bad that I wasn't getting any attention at home so she decided to help. She was also glad that I was working on my marriage. Then she got up, pecked me on the cheek, said she was going to miss me because I was the sweetest man she'd ever dated, and then she left. I admired her for her maturity, but that was it.

With time, life began to improve. I spent time studying the word of God. I got a promotion at work, we moved into our own house, and I bought a new car for Marissa. Life was indeed good.

Then one day, I was at work on a fine afternoon when there was a knock at the door.

"Come in, please," I said without looking up from my work.

The door opened, someone stepped in and cleared their throat. I looked up, standing there was Rahim. I forced myself to be calm and motioned for him to sit.

"Thanks, man." He said as he sat down.

"How may I help you?" I asked him, looking into his eyes.

"Greg, I don't know what I'll say now to erase what happened, there are not enough words to quantify my regret, but please forgive me. Please."

I remembered what my Pastor had said and I let out a sigh. "It's okay, Rahim. I forgive you." I smiled.

"Thanks a lot, man, I appreciate this." He looked happy.

"You're welcome. And I'm sorry for hitting you," I said.

"I deserved it, Greg." We both became quiet. I'm sure it was because we were both thinking about the same thing, that day at his house.

"So, how is your family?" I asked, breaking the silence.

"Well, fine," he said, a huge grin on his face. "My wife finally grew some spunk and told me where to shove it."

I laughed aloud. "Really? Good for her." I was still laughing.

"Yeah, she left me for some time," he said. I stopped laughing immediately.

"Oh, I'm sorry."

"No, she's back, though. After much pleading with promises to change, she came back. Now things are different. I help her around the house, I go home early. I even go to church now with her and the kids."

"Wow, that's wonderful. Rahim, I'm so glad." I was genuinely happy for him.

"Thanks. I knew I had to make up with you and now that I have, my joy is full," he said.

"Wow, same here, man." I walked around my desk and hugged him tightly. We both sniffed audibly. We talked some more and then he left. I sat alone in my office, thinking about everything that had just happened. I was glad that Rahim had repented.

I looked at the time and it was noon. I didn't care. I shut down my computer, locked up and rushed out of my office.

"Boss, are you going out?" My secretary asked, surprised. I never left the office this early.

"I'm going home to my wife," I yelled as I ran out of the office.

I jumped into my car and sped to Marissa's shop. I called her when I was close and told her to come out. She was waiting outside when I got there.

"Get in," I commanded.

"What's going on?" She was puzzled, and then she saw my face. There was an instant understanding.

"Ohhh." She smiled shyly and got in quickly, giggling.

Luckily, her shop wasn't too far from our house and in no time we were home. We got out of the car simultaneously and hurried to the door. As it shut behind us, we started kissing. We kissed passionately, rushing it, then we slowed down drinking in each other's essence, our tongues intertwining every now and then. I kissed Marissa, my wife, with every emotion I had abandoned for so long. I sucked at her lower lip and ran the tip of my tongue over it.

"Oh my," she said into my mouth and I laughed.

When we could take it no longer, I took Marissa upstairs and made good love to her. I tried to make up for the past two months that I hadn't touched her. I worshipped her from the crown of her head to the soles of her feet, in a way that I'd never done before. I knew that I had her for life when tears of joy began to flow from her eyes. She held on to me tightly and told me that she loved me with all of her heart and soul. I told her that I loved her more. And I meant it.

She was the essence of my being, everything within me was hers, and my life was inside of her. Because she was my wife. I had no other choice than to love her, God had commanded me to. Whether I felt it or not, I had to because love is not a feeling, it's a conscious decision you make to be kind to your wife, no matter what. That was what I understood by Ephesians 5:25, which says, "Husbands, love your wives, just as Christ loved the church and gave Himself up for her."

So here I was, loving my wife with revelation knowledge, having understood the mystery of one flesh. If I did anything to myself, I would be doing it to my wife as well. If I cheated, she would cheat as well, whether physically or emotionally. If I abused her emotionally, physically, verbally or sexually, I would be doing all that to myself. Whatever I did with my body, I would be doing to hers as well. It was so simple and I was glad that I'd gotten divine knowledge from God. I was no longer confused. My path was as clear as daylight.

That night, we decided to renew our vows, and a month later, we stood before our Pastor and a few family and friends to do the same. Marissa looked beautiful in a cream, nicely cut dress, and I was dashing in a black, three-piece suit. Marissa had said that I looked like a prince.

So we renewed our vows in the presence of our folks.

"You may now kiss the bride" Pastor directed and I did, with great fervor.

The broken hedge had been replanted by the only one who could. Jesus Christ, The Word!

# 2

# A Price To Pay

***Dedicated to:***

HAVILAH GOLD AND MANY OTHERS
WHO ESCAPED. FOR FIN.
FOR EVERY WOMAN GOING THROUGH ABUSE.

"Come on baby, just look at it. It's beautiful and sleek, just like you. I got it for you because I knew you would like it. It's the Samsung Galaxy Note 5!" He was sitting beside her on the bed, his shoulder touching hers, his tone imploring. He took her hand and placed the phone in it.

Remi looked at her husband, Akin, through the swollen slits of her eyes and started to smile, but her lips were stiff, and the pain wouldn't let her. So, instead, she grimaced and nodded. She couldn't smile, nor could she speak. It was too painful to do so.

"Baby, honestly, I'm terribly sorry. I don't know what came over me. I know I've said this many times before now but I promise that this is the last time. I will never hit you again, okay?"

She stared at the phone in her hand, her mind in a state of nothingness. She had stopped feeling, resigned to the fact that she was created to be this man's punching bag. She knew he would do it again. She knew it. It was her fate. No one was going to live it for her. It was all on her.

She looked at him again and nodded. "Thank you," she croaked.

"It's nothing, baby. Anything for you." He brought her free hand to his lips and kissed it. Then he began to unbutton her blouse.

She shivered as his fingers brushed against her bruised skin.

"Are you cold? Don't worry, I'll warm you up in a minute." He smiled at her. He did not think to turn off the air conditioner that was blasting out cold air.

He went on to take off her clothes and started to caress her.

She whimpered. Her whole body hurt like hell. But she did not try to stop him. She allowed him to kiss her body, even though each touch of his lips hurt her. She choked back a yell as he rested his weight on her, parted her legs and in one powerful movement slid into her. The tears burned behind her eyes.

"Baby, I'm sorry okay? It stops now. It stops today. Never again. I won't ever hit you again, babe. Oh, you're so sweet, baby," he murmured huskily as he moved in and out of her.

She felt shame deep inside because she began to enjoy the movement of his penis inside her. She moaned and his thrusts became harder and faster. And then he slowed it down and began to grind his groin against hers.

"Oh, Akin!" She screamed in pleasure, all hurt forgotten as she felt herself exploding.

"Yeah baby," he groaned, coming with her.

A moment later, he rolled off of her and got out the bed.

"I'm hungry. Get up and fix dinner, okay?" he hissed as he walked into the adjoining bathroom.

She turned on her side, curled into a tight ball of pain and shame, and let the tears flow.

---

REMI PEERED INTO the mirror, her eyes fixed on the huge bruise on her right cheek. She needed to cover it up before she could get downstairs. She knew couldn't hide in her room forever. She was hungry, she had to eat. She wouldn't have bothered leaving her room otherwise. Not with the bruise so noticeable on her cheek.

She zipped open her cosmetic bag and emptied its contents onto the dresser. Then she reached for her foundation tube and gently began to apply it to her face. She looked at her work in the mirror, there was still a dark spot. She applied some concealer directly onto it, hoping that it would hide the spread of discoloration, and when she was done, she dabbed on some loose powder.

Feeling satisfied that she had done a good job of covering it up, she peered closely in the mirror again but shuddered at the absurd inconsistency of her efforts. Her left cheek was absolutely normal while the right one looked fake and cakey.

She sighed in frustration and reached for some wipes and cleaned up her entire face. Food would have to wait. She was in no state to be seen yet. She was going to need a few days.

She stared at her reflection in the mirror and realised how well she had adjusted to the pattern. She would look perfectly normal one minute, and the next, her face would be so swollen you would think that she had been in a boxing match. She had had to quit her job because it eventually got to a point where the number of times she called in sick became too ridiculous to her own ears, let alone her boss's. So, she had given up her career altogether to avoid being known as the person with the poorest work ethic in the world.

Akin had been overjoyed when she told him she was thinking of giving up her career. He had only allowed her to work because her father had gotten her the job. He was a very jealous man, who was always paranoid about other men being around her. Actually, he was jealous of everyone around her. She had no friends because of that. And since she was an only child, there were no siblings for her to be close with. He had sworn to provide all of her needs just so she could stay at home. And he did. She had everything any woman could want; the best of clothes, shoes, jewellery, cosmetics, mobile devices and an array of ridiculously expensive lingerie which he made her wear each time they had sex.

Despite having all these things, she had no freedom to enjoy them because she was unhappy most of the time. Whenever Akin deemed it an appropriate punishment for something she had done wrong, he would take everything away from her and would only return them after she apologized and they made up. It happened so many times that eventually, all the good stuff came to mean nothing to her.

And so it was that she became a miserable and often beaten and battered housewife who took care of her husband and their home. They had no children. They had tried for five years since the day they were married. So, with resignation and sometimes relief on Remi's part, it had been her and Akin until recently when he announced that his younger sister, Busola was coming to live with them. They had his brother, Dotun over every now and then, but Busola had come to stay.

## Busola.

She was the second person Remi knew whom Akin was wary of. The first person was Akin's maternal aunt, Folashade whom Busola had gone to live with when she was just three-years-old, right after their mother died. Akin was fifteen at the time. He had just completed secondary school and was about to go to university. Dotun, who was a very independent eight-year-old, on the other hand, had remained with their father. It was agreed that Busola should live with Aunty Folashade because she was very young and because she was a girl.

Remi had no idea why her husband was wary of Busola because she had never really spent time with her. All she really knew about her was a result of the little that her husband, Akin had told her. And according to his version of Busola, she was aggressive, opinionated and bold, just like their Aunty Folashade. All the things that Akin hated in a woman.

"I don't like it. I don't like it one bit, but she is my kid sister, so I have to let her come and stay with us. But you will do well to stay away from her and keep our business out of her ears. Is that understood?" Akin had warned and Remi had nodded in agreement.

So, Busola, at twenty-one and fresh out of university had come to live with them indefinitely. She wanted to get to know her brother as they had been apart for most of their lives. She had arrived a couple of weeks ago, but they rarely spoke to each other. Remi made sure to avoid Busola's inquisitive and piercing stare whenever they happened to bump into each other in the house. She would quickly find an excuse to leave Busola's presence because she did not want any trouble from Akin.

So, instead of finally having a sister to talk to, Remi was always cooped up in her own room, away from her.

On the other hand, she had been more relaxed with Dotun because he never asked any questions. He was a very calm boy who was always so kind to her. Remi couldn't help but recall how glad she had been when Dotun first started to visit them. She had thought she would finally have company whenever Akin was at work. She had also erroneously believed that the beatings would cease. She had been wrong. Barely a few days after Dotun arrived, Akin had given her the beating of her life for daring to wave at their next door neighbour, Mr. Desmond. He had accused her of throwing herself at Mr. Desmond. He had deafened his ears to Dotun's cries of plea on her behalf and warned him sternly to get out of their business and stay out of it.

"Listen here, young man. If you want to have peace whenever you are in this house, you must learn to keep your nose out of my business. What I choose to do with *my* wife is none of *your* concern," he had roared viciously. The poor boy had retreated to his room only to come out much later when Akin had stormed out of the house.

Dotun had knocked at her door; at first softly and later loudly, and begged her to open up so he could take care of her wounds but she had assured him through the locked door and swollen lips that she was okay. And from then on she had known her fate. Her parents were not helpful either because they kept sending her back to Akin every time she ran to them for protection.

"You are from a Christian home, and Christian women don't abandon their husbands," her father had said to her the first time she had run home. "You must learn to be submissive to him like your mother is to me so that he will stop beating you. He is not your mate so you must keep your mouth shut whenever he is talking. You must carry out your duties with respect. Do not bring shame to this family, so do not come back here again with this nonsense!" Her mother had stood behind him, nodding sagely at each word he'd thrown at Remi.

A colleague of her father's, Akin had married her fresh out of an all girls' Christian university. She had just turned twenty-two at the time and was still a virgin. She had stared in awe at the huge handsome man, fifteen years older than her, who had come to her house every weekend bearing gifts for her and her mother. Akin had already made his intentions known to her father, so every time he visited, her parents would leave the two of them alone in the living room to talk. She had marvelled at Akin's of knowledge almost everything. His interests, intellectual finesse, and his great charm, had captured her heart firmly. She had never known anyone quite like him, except in the romance novels that she had hidden in her room to read well after her parents had gone to bed.

She had fallen for him; hopelessly and completely. She had crumbled like the work of a dubious architect, and within a few months, they had gotten married.

Everything had been heavenly; the wedding, the honeymoon, the gifts and the pampering. And all the doubts she had had about fairy tales had disappeared because of the incredible ways in which Akin showed her love. Until the first time that he hit her.

She had been asleep one night when he shook her awake to go get him some water from downstairs and she had mumbled something about how tired she was and that he should go and get it himself. The sharp smack across her face had roused her. Even ice cold water could not have instantly awakened her like that first slap. She had sat up in bed, shocked, her hand on her throbbing cheek.

"You slapped me!" She had whispered incredulously as tears gathered in her eyes. He had then dragged her out of the bed and rained more blows on her all the while yelling for his water. She had run out of their bedroom and down the stairs in bewilderment, shock, and fear, with him in hot pursuit. He did not stop hitting her until she had filled a glass with water and stretched it out to him.

He had apologised profusely afterwards, fervently promising never to hit her again. She had believed him. She had believed him countless times after that, over and over and over again until it eventually dawned on her that he would never be able to stop beating her. So, whenever he apologised, she just accepted it mechanically.

---

SHE LOVED HIM but feared him. She dreaded the end of every day because she knew that he would come home to her. He never slept outside their home except for business and he always took her with him. She never spoke to him unless he required it of her. She had no idea what would trigger the beast in him, so she only responded to his questions and she thought carefully before she spoke. She never asked him for anything, she never got the chance to for he was generous with gifts. He always provided what he believed she liked. She never went out except with him. He made her write a list of the things they needed in the house and had someone from his office do the shopping for her. He found her a good hairdresser who came to the house every fortnight to make her hair so she was pretty much all by herself. And he never gave her money.

They stopped going to church after their pastor started a weekly series on the dangers of wife battery and abuse. Akin had cursed the pastor on their way home that day, calling him a fake man of God, and promising to find them another church to attend. That was a year ago. And because she did not want to find herself in trouble, she had taken to watching Christian channels on cable.

She knew that she would never be safe from her husband's abuse. It was her fate and no one could save her from it. She lived like a prisoner in her own home. Daring to go against his rules and regulations - and he had lots of them - would mean incurring his wrath, so she yielded all the time. She never thought of getting out because she knew not how. She had grown tired of praying about it because of all the prayers she had said, none got answered.

One night, a couple of months ago, she had prayed again. It had been a single, heartfelt cry for freedom and she had felt peace in her heart afterwards. She had been so certain that God had finally heard her. She waited for a few days for the manifestation, but as the days flew into months and there was no sign of an angel from above, she had given up and continued with her life. So she didn't pray anymore.

She sighed again and rose abruptly from the stool on which she had been sitting. She quickly grabbed on the table as she felt the room spin. She remembered again that she had not had anything to eat since the previous day, hence the dizziness. She had however taken in a lot of fluids, even though she knew that was not enough to sustain her anymore. She decided to throw caution to the wind and go downstairs to make herself some lunch.

A nice aroma wafted into her nostrils as she climbed down the stairs, and she heard movement in the kitchen. It was Dotun in there. He liked being in the kitchen a lot. Remi's steps began to falter as she heard another voice; Busola's, but the rumbling in her stomach propelled her forward.

"Sis Remi! Good afternoon ma." Dotun's greeting was warm and effusive as Remi walked into the kitchen.

"Good afternoon, ma'am," Busola calmly greeted.

Busola was tall and big-boned, just like Akin. Despite her size, she was smart and very quick on her feet. She was also very pretty, with the sharpest pair of eyes Remi had ever seen on any face.

"Good afternoon, guys. What's going on here?" her stomach grumbled at the dish of steaming rice and very red stew on the kitchen table.

"I found some stew in the freezer so I heated it and boiled some rice," Busola explained with a defiant look on her face.

"That's nice. Thanks." Remi smiled at her.

"You are welcome! Do you want to eat now? I'll dish you some." Busola offered.

"Oh, don't worry, I'll get it myself," she said, but Busola moved quickly to the counter and removed a plate from the rack.

"Just sit down and I'll serve you." She smiled.

Remi stared at Busola and marvelled at her sweetness. It was hard to believe the things Akin had said about her. She almost wanted to refuse but doing that would hurt Busola's feelings so she smiled at her and sat at the table instead.

"Okay, Busola. Thank you." Her heart felt a little lighter and she settled in her seat.

Remi smiled and thanked Busola again when she placed her food in front of her.

"Enough with the thanks already! You are too ... aargh!" Busola said, rolling her eyes in exasperation.

"What? Is it a crime to be appreciative of someone's niceness?" Remi was puzzled.

"See, sister Remi once is enough. Also, I'm not always nice, so don't get used to it. I just figured you would need some nutrients after that beating your husband gave you yesterday. I won't do this tomorrow!"

"Busola!" Dotun was appalled

"What?" Busola queried.

"It's fine," Remi said, feeling nauseated. She nevertheless dug into her meal.

They ate in silence for a while and then Dotun asked, "How's your eye, Sis Remi?"

"Oh, my eye is fine, thanks," Remi answered, smiling a little too brightly.

"Doesn't look fine to me. It still looks swollen. Are you sure it's fine?" Busola's sharp eyes bored into hers.

"I'm sure," Remi answered, feeling uneasy.

"Okay." She didn't sound convinced.

Remi picked at her food, her appetite gone as she became very conscious of Busola's knowing eyes on her.

"So what do you do for fun, Sis Remi?" Busola asked.

"Fun? Well, I watch movies, and I play games," Remi answered cautiously.

"Hmmm. Are you on Facebook?" Busola asked.

"Yes, I am"

"Wow! That's great! I will send you a friend request right away." Busola picked up her phone.

"Okay." Remi bit her lip nervously.

"What's your profile name?"

"Em ... Mrs Akin Peters, I think."

"Huh? Mrs Akin Peters, you think? Wait, did he open the account for you?"

"Yes, he did! And he has the password too. Happy now?"

"Well, I'll be ... Why, sister Remi?" She asked suddenly.

"Why what?" Remi asked guardedly.

"Why do you put up with this abuse?"

"Busola, please mind your business in this house. Don't cause problems for sister Remi," Dotun cut in.

"Go grind some pepper, Dotun. You think you are doing her good by buttering her up? Keeping mute about the evil your damn brother is doing? Oh no, you are not! If she dies by his hands, you would have caused her death. Why? Because you refused to speak up, so join me on this, okay? Sis Remi, you know it's wrong. You know he is a beast who can very well kill you one day. Why do you put up with it? What is keeping you here still? You have no kids, else I would understand why you are still here, although that's not enough reason to remain with a violent man. So, why? You deserve far more than this and you know it. I can't promise you that I would understand but just tell me why!" Busola ranted.

"He is my husband and I promised to stay with him for better or worse," Remi answered lamely.

"Oh, please!" Busola laughed sarcastically.

"Do not mock me, Busola. This is my house and what happens between my husband and me is none of your business so stay out of it!" Remi said angrily, dropping her spoon and rising to her feet.

"It is my business because you are first and foremost a human being, and I have a responsibility to protect my fellow human being." Busola returned as she rose with her.

"Protect me? You think you can protect me from him?" it was her turn to throw a sarcastic laugh.

"Yes, I can. I must, and other than carting you off on my back I will talk some sense into you because you certainly have lost it."

"How dare you!" Remi spat, looking angry and hurt.

"Now, that came out wrong and I'm sorry but it basically sums up my thoughts."

Remi shook her head in disbelief. She knew she it was time for her to stomp off but she just couldn't. She felt a kind of stirring in her heart at her sister-in-law's words.

Busola sighed and moved towards Remi.

"I'm very sorry, sister Remi. It's just that I'm so mad at my brother for being such a beast and at you for taking the abuse. It hurts me. It reminds me of how it was with my parents."

"What? Your parents? Why? What happened with your parents?" Remi asked with surprise.

"You mean he didn't tell you? Of course, he wouldn't." She said bitterly.

"Tell me, please."

"I will tell you. But first, you need to start looking to get out of this bondage. I thank the Lord that you came downstairs today, that you even sat in my presence for more than a minute that you are even listening to me. I am truly grateful for that. I am glad that I have this shot at reaching out to you. I want to help you, please. Will you allow me to help you?"

Remi looked at Busola with great mirth, wondering how she hoped to help her. She was also intrigued. She couldn't resist taking a long peek into the new world that Busola had formed in her mind. A world of freedom.

"Please, tell me about your parents, Busola." Remi pleaded.

Busola's eyes darkened with pain as she began...

"I was little then so I didn't know much but I remember some stuff and Aunty Folashade filled me in on the rest. I remember feeling sad all the time because my mother was always sad. He beat her all the time, over little or nothing, and there was no one to help her save for Aunty Folashade. But she was hooked on to him, despite Aunty's attempts to pull her out of his hold. Brother Akin was mature enough to know better and try to stop the abuse but he didn't because he idolised our father, so it went on for years until the last time he beat her. This time, she sustained blows to her ribs and clavicle but she didn't go to the hospital, so she was unaware that she was bleeding internally. She died from internal bleeding three days later..."

"Oh my God!" Remi felt faint.

Busola gave a sad smile and continued.

"Aunty Folashade was heartbroken. She blamed herself for not doing more. She still blames herself until today. She tried to make up for the loss by being there for me all these years, bringing me up in the best way possible and I am grateful for who I am. And even though she isn't really tender and loving, the way a mommy usually is, she did a great job raising me and I don't want to be anyone else."

"Oh my God!" Remi was crying now.

"So you see, sister Remi? You see why I can't leave you alone now? I can't have you die on my watch like my mother did on Aunty Folashade's. I want to help you get your freedom. Please, let me help you!' Busola begged.

"Oh, I feel so sad for your mom. And for you. You were just a baby! Even you, Dotun." Remi looked forlorn.

"Yeah, sister Remi, it wasn't pleasant at all. Do you ladies mind? I'm going to my room." Dotun looked grim as he walked out of the kitchen.

"That's in the past, Sis Remi. This is now. This is the time to act, to change your life, to free you forever! Don't tell me you enjoy the way you live. Do you like this house that much?"

"What? I hate this house. I hate my room." Remi said quietly.

"Okay..."

"That's where he beats me. Always. That is where he defiles my spirit." Her voice was low.

"Why are you always cooped up in there then?" Busola asked softly.

'It's familiar. It's all I know.' Remi stared at nothingness as she narrated to Busola some of the harrowing experiences she had endured at her husband's hands.

"Oh damn!" Busola's heart ached deeply. She had to restrain herself from marching to Akin's office and punching him in the face.

"It's pathetic, right?" Remi smiled sadly.

"No, dear. It's not pathetic. It's just sad. A shame, really, because you shouldn't be going through this. You shouldn't be having this experience. No one should." Busola touched her arm.

"But *I* am. And I think I must have done something really terrible to have this happening to me..." Remi said, her smile wry.

"What? No, there's nothing you could have done in the past to deserve this. It's not your fault that you married a beast who lacks self-control. You did no crime marrying a man who made you believe that he loved you and would never hurt you. But the only crime you are committing now is staying with the beast and putting up with the abuse. If you really want to make restitution for whatever wrong you believe you did in the past, you must leave him!" Busola said with vehemence.

"I don't know how..."

"I do. I will help you leave him. I will help you run away."

"I have nowhere to run to..." she replied.

"Oh, I know a place, sister Remi! I know a place where you will be safe, forever. No more fear, no more sadness and no more pain. A place where you can heal from all the pain he has inflicted on you."

"He will kill me; he will kill you. He hates betrayal, especially from the people who are close to him. Like me, like you. He will kill us. Are you willing to die for someone who is not even your blood?"

"Yes! I will die to liberate you, and if you are not, I will come back and die for you again and again. It's the path I have chosen for myself. It's for my late mother's sake, it's for your sake, and for the sake of our daughters and sisters all over the world. I have pledged my life to the freedom and service of women who are as bound as you are. You can't dissuade me from doing this so I think we should start planning!"

"Okay. But if he knows about this, we are dead!" She said with dread.

"So we pretend that we hate each other's guts until the plan is hatched. The only thing that will disrupt this plan is if he beats you again. I will never stand for that, so please, be safe. Okay?"

"Well, okay. If you are sure it will work…" Remi still couldn't believe the possibility of gaining her freedom.

"It will, believe me. As a matter of fact, it will be so easy because we know his schedule. We will strike when he's at work!" Busola grinned.

"That's true, Busola! So you mean that after five years of pain I will finally be free? Wait, what about my parents? What about money? We are going to need money!" Remi frowned.

"Forget about your parents! Why should you bother? It's not as if they care whether you are alive or not. It's obvious they don't care. Please, just forget about them for now. You can contact them much later. As for money, don't worry. Everything is available where we are going. Just come as you are." Busola assured.

"Wow! Okay. I will be twenty-seven next week and I will finally be free!" Remi exclaimed happily.

"Yes. I have a great idea! We will run away on your birthday!" Busola said with eyes alight.

"What a great birthday present! Thank you Busola." Remi hugged Busola tightly.

---

THE LAST FEW days before her birthday were the most exciting days of Remi's entire life. As soon as Akin left for work each morning, she would join Busola downstairs and they would talk about domestic violence. Busola would bring her computer and they would visit websites that talked about domestic violence. Remi became convinced that she deserved her freedom, that she would no longer be a prisoner.

Then as evening approached, Remi would go back upstairs and pretend that she had not stepped foot downstairs all day.

That weekend, Dotun went back to his station and the two young women were by themselves during the day. They had lots of fun and Remi began to feel like she finally had a sister.

In a brief moment of sobriety, Remi asked, "what of God, Busola? God said He hates divorce…"

"He sure did. He also said He hates violence. Let me tell you something, Remi, God loves marriage but He loves the people in it more." Busola countered.

Everything was going smoothly until the night before her birthday. Akin announced that he was taking her out of town for her birthday.

'No!' She cried in panic.

'What?" Akin frowned at her suspiciously.

"Oh, I mean, I would like to spend the day at home. I don't feel like going anywhere for my birthday." She stuttered.

"Hmmm. You don't want to spend time with me?" His tone was angry, his mouth tight.

"Oh no, baby. That's not what I meant. Please, forget what I said. Let's go wherever you want us to go." She tried desperately to repair the damage of her words. If he so much as detected anything, she was dead.

"Hmmm." His sharp eyes pierced into hers, but she managed to hold his stare, even though her mind was in a turmoil.

"Let's do it, please," she smiled at him coyly, and his lips thinned even more.

She forgot that she was supposed to be a submissive wife, not a coy one.

"Okay. You can pack your stuff tonight. We will leave in the morning" he said lightly and she silently released the breath she had been holding.

"Okay," was her quiet response.

That night, she packed her things in agitation. She had to find a way to tell Busola that their plan had been disrupted. She had no business downstairs anymore that night so she knew no way to tell her. She didn't have Busola's phone number and even if she did, she never touched her phone when her husband was home; unless she had an incoming call. That was one of his many rules.

She was almost going crazy when Akin said to her he felt like having a light snack and asked her to put something together for him.

"I don't mind at all," she said almost too enthusiastically, jumping to her feet and racing downstairs before he could blink.

As she trotted down the stairs, she spied a light from the living room, so she tip-toed in there and stood by the door. Busola was lying on the sofa, her eyes glued to the TV.

"Pssst!" Busola turned to her and Remi motioned her over. Busola scrambled to her feet and rushed towards her.

"What's the matter?" Busola whispered.

"The plan. We need to abort the plan. He wants us to go away tomorrow!" Remi whispered back.

"No!" Busola exclaimed in disbelief.

"Yes! We have to put it off for now. I need to go make him a snack."

"Dammit!" Busola swore as she watched Remi hurry away.

She stood there for a while, thinking about how eerie things were turning. She felt like she was in a horror movie because there were goosebumps all over her body. She sighed and turned to go back to watching her show and was startled to see Akin standing behind her.

"Brother! Ah, you scared me!" She laughed nervously, wondering how much he had heard.

"Sorry. What was that about?" he asked.

"Oh, she wanted to know who was in here," Busola said as she walked back into the living room. She grabbed the remote and sunk into one of the single seats.

"Hmmm. I need you to do something for me tomorrow morning. I need to go into the office first thing but I will be back before noon. I need you to watch her for me. She's up to something. I can feel it." He said rapidly.

"What? That mouse? She's got no game, bro. She's all about you! You have nothing to worry about." Busola tried to be light, but she actually wanted to punch him in the face.

"Listen to me, I know her inside out and I know she is different. Just keep your eye on her tomorrow and never let her out of your sight. Call me the moment you notice any funny business." And with that, he walked out of the room.

Busola smiled inwardly. Akin had just presented to her the getaway car and she was behind the wheel. As soon as he left for his frigging office, they would strike.

The next morning broke clear and bright. It was a beautiful day to be free. True to his words, Akin left the house at exactly 8:00 a.m. Busola peered through the blinds to be sure that the gate had shut behind him. She waited for about twenty minutes and then raced upstairs to get Remi. She found her sitting on the bed, twirling her fingers nervously.

"He's gone, let's go!" She urged, but Remi just looked the more worried.

"Sister Remi. It is time." Busola held her gaze.

"Busola, I don't know if this is a good idea. I have a feeling that he knows something." Remi squeaked.

"He suspects something and that's why we need to get going. I will explain on the way." Busola said urgently.

"I don't know how, Busola. I don't know!" She started to cry.

"I know. I understand. But you need to know. You need to stay alive so you can know. You need to know so you can help others. Please..." Busola said softly and extended her hand to Remi.

There was something in Busola's eyes that gave Remi courage and at that moment she believed all over again.

"Okay!" She placed her hand in Busola's and allowed herself to be pulled up and together they ran downstairs. As they reached the foot of the stairs, Remi suddenly stopped.

"Wait! I saw some money upstairs, a whole case of it. I want to take it."

"I told you we don't need his money. I have enough..."

"Busola, I am NOT leaving this house with nothing! Not after all I have been through!" Remi said rigidly.

"Okay, go and get it. But please hurry!" Busola was worried. She had amazingly strong intuition and it was screaming danger.

Remi dashed back upstairs and in a flash she was back, holding a large briefcase.

"I got it, Busola," she grinned in triumph.

"Great! Now let's get out of this dump."

Busola led them out of the mansion and into the compound where her car was parked. Remi opened the back door and flung the suitcase onto the back seat. She slammed the door shut and stood for a moment, looking around the compound with a grim expression.

"Get in!" Busola was already at the wheel and she watched as Remi spat on the ground, yanked the passenger's side door open and jumped inside.

Busola reversed the car recklessly and drove towards the gate with her hand hard pressed on the horn. But a whole minute passed and Tunde, the security guard didn't come out.

She honked the horn another full minute, still, there was no response. And she knew that something was off.

She looked at Remi and smiled reassuringly. She couldn't afford to fail the broken woman sitting beside her.

"Let me see what's going on with Tunde," she said brightly as she opened her door.

"I'll come with you." Remi opened hers too and they got out

the same time. They walked hand in hand toward the gatehouse and stood before the door.

"Tunde?" Busola knocked hard but there was no answer so she turned the knob and pushed open the door.

Just as she had suspected, Busola stared into the eyes of her brother, Akin.

"Going somewhere?" He scowled. Remi gasped in terror, turned on her heel and began to run back into the house.

"No, Remi, come back! Don't go in there. Get in the car!" Busola screamed after Remi's retreating back but it was too late. Remi had fled into the house.

That ruined her plan. She would have rammed the car into Akin if he had tried to stop them. Not enough to kill him but to wound him or throw him off balance. They could have escaped easily after that.

"Busola!" Akin barked at her, his face a mask of anger.

"Yes, Brother?" she maintained her brave stand.

"You? My own sister? Plottng with my wife against me? My own flesh and blood betraying me?" he said through gritted teeth.

"Brother, you are a violent husband. You beat her every..."

"Shut up, you little brat! I knew it! I knew it was a big mistake bringing you into my house. I should never have allowed you to come here. Now, you will go inside, pack your stuff and get out of my house!"

"I will not..."

"Oh yes, you will, Miss! You are leaving here and I never want to see your face again"

"Hell, I want to leave this stupid house too. But not without Remi. She is coming with me!" Busola faced him.

"What? Do you want to steal my wife from me? My own wife? After all that I have done for you?"

"What did you do for me, Brother? Please, tell me what you did to make my life bearable after Mommy died. Tell me how many times you came looking for me after I went to live with Aunty Fola. Please, tell me..."

"I offered to pay your tuition..."

"But you didn't! See, that is not even the point. The point is that you are abusing a woman like me, you are violent to her and I cannot stand by and let that happen," she stated.

"Busola, this is your last warning. Leave my house now!"

"No, I am not leaving, not without Remi"

"Okay. Go and rescue her then." Akin nodded towards the house, his voice full of menace.

Busola eyed him for a moment, then she turned and walked back into the house. Once she was inside, she started to call out to Remi, but there was no answer so she raced upstairs and burst through their bedroom door. Remi was crouched in a corner, her face in a mask of fear.

"Remi, come on, let's go!" Busola went to her and grabbed her arm.

"No! He's here. He will kill us. I told you he was smart, Busola. He caught us, it's over!" Remi whispered in panic. Her fear-filled eyes were glued to the door.

"No, it's not over! We can still leave. You just need to get over your fear and stand with me, Remi!"

"I am scared! I can't!" Remi sobbed loudly.

"Well, I can, and I am not leaving without you. I can't leave you in this house."

"Don't leave me, please. I can't leave but don't leave me. Stay here with me, please. I don't care if he keeps beating me, I just want you here, please!"

"Yes, you can leave him! And I care that he beats you. Remi, we can't remain here. We should not remain here; we don't have to..."

Remi thought about how terrible the situation was. She didn't know how she could walk out on her husband. She didn't know how she could watch Busola walk away...

"Remi, you have a whole new life waiting for you. You deserve a whole new life. You don't deserve one moment of needless and avoidable pain or uncertainty. You need to live in a world where you won't have to walk on eggshells or look over your shoulders anymore."

Remi knew that Busola was right. She was just twenty-six, but it felt like her life was over. She had no future with Akin. She was not happy with him. She would never be fulfilled if she stayed. Besides, now that he was aware of her plans to leave him, he would make things worse for her. She could not bear to live that way with him anymore. She had to leave with Busola. She needed to leave.

"You are right, Busola. I will stand with you. I want a new life. I deserve it!" Remi stated firmly as she rose to her feet.

"Good! So let's go."

Remi was still scared, but with Busola by her side, she felt stronger, braver. As they walked down the stairs together, Akin was there by the front door waiting for them.

"We are leaving, Brother."

"Is that so? I told you before, Busola, you can leave for all I care. I will gladly pay you to leave, but my wife is going nowhere. This is where she belongs, this is her home and her life. I suggest that you go and find yours."

"You call this a life? She is locked up all day, every day, she gets beaten all the time, she has no opinion, she dares not have a mind of her own, no friends, no social life of her own. Nothing! This is no life!" Busola cried.

"You are just jealous, Busola, and I won't bother with that. Please, let go of my wife and get out of here!"

"No! I am going with Busola!" Remi found her voice.

"What?" Akin was in shock.

"You heard me. I am leaving this house. I can't stay here anymore." Her voice was shaky, but she successfully got the words out.

"You are leaving me? You can't leave me! You belong to me forever. Now, get back upstairs this minute!" Akin roared and Remi took a step back, shivering in fear.

"Stop being such a bully and get out of our way! Look at you, living your father's life all over again. This is how he treated Mommy and you did nothing about it even though you could." Busola spat.

"What is my business with how a man runs his home? It was daddy's home to run so I had no business in it. No one should interfere in other people's marriage!" Akin defended.

"That is a load of hogwash. There are exceptions to that rule, Akin. You don't ignore a man who abuses his wife. You never do that. You speak out. She was your mother, Akin. How come you could bear it for one moment, let alone years? How come you didn't have any compassion for your own mother? How come you were able to watch her get beat up and ridiculed all the time and not do anything about it?"

"Busola that is not the point! You are totally veering towards untroubled waters."

"Oh, you think that is untroubled waters? She died, Akin! She died from his abuse and nothing was done about it. She got no justice. And I was robbed of my mother's love. I grew up without my mom! She never knew fulfilment. She was a sad woman all of her life. She had no chance and she died a pointless death, Akin. If you feel nothing about that then you truly are a beast, like your father!" Busola's eyes spat fire, but she was not prepared for the slap that landed on her face.

"No!" Remi screamed and moved back to Busola's side.

"How dare you speak about our father like that?" Akin breathed the words in fury.

"Akin, you dared to raise your hand against me..." Busola smiled menacingly at him.

"I had to keep you in check. You were going way out of line. Now, enough of this nonsense! Get out! And you, Remi, get back upstairs, now!!!"

"No! I am not going upstairs and Busola is not leaving without me. I will not remain in this house with you any minute longer. I was blind but now I got my sight back. I won't live here anymore. I am done!" Remi spat at him.

Akin threw his head back and laughed wickedly.

"Oh, now you are bold like Busola, right? She has rubbed off on you and you want to show off to me, right? If you weren't so pathetic, it would be funny. Yes, that's what you are, pathetic! Now get upstairs this instant!" He yanked Remi away from

Busola and pushed her towards the stairs. Remi stumbled and landed face down on the tiled floor.

"Remi!" Busola shrieked in fright and ran to her. She tried to lift Remi to her feet but Remi's almost still form made it difficult.

"I am okay, Busola." Remi winced in pain as she got up.

"What the hell is wrong with you?" Busola threw herself at Akin. She pushed him in the chest, yelling colourful expletives at him.

"Busola, stop! Don't fight him. Don't let him make you less than you are. Let's just go, please..." Remi pleaded and Busola sighed and moved back from Akin.

'Remi, you are not going anywhere. You are not leaving me. You are not leaving me alone in this house.'

"Akin, I can't live this way anymore. I need to breathe and I can't do that here. I need to leave."

"You need to breathe? You can open the windows and let in some air. We don't need to use the AC all the time. We can..."

"'No, Akin. That's not what I mean and you know it. I need to live. I don't want to end up like your mother." Remi stated.

"You!" Akin growled and lunged himself at Busola.

"Akin, leave her alone!" Remi yelled, clawing at his back. He elbowed her off his back and she fell down. He wrapped his large hands around Busola's neck and started to squeeze.

"Stop it!" Remi had gotten back to her feet and was hitting him on his back, causing him to loosen his hold on Busola's neck.

"I am coming to you next, Remi, my dear wife. I will get to you in a minute," he said through gritted teeth.

Busola tried to speak but she started coughing instead, her eyes bulging out of their sockets. Akin pushed her away from him and turned to face his wife.

"Last chance, Remi. Get upstairs!" His eyes were in slits.

"No, please. I don't want to." Remi's voice shook with fear. She was truly afraid. Busola was down so she was pretty much on her own. She knew she could not withstand her husband's brute strength.

"I can't let you leave me, Remi. I built my life around you. I can't live with any other woman but you. So I'm not letting you go. Not now, not ever. Unless one of us dies..."

'Akin, do you have any idea how many times I have died in this house, in your hands? I had nothing in me anymore until your sister came into my life. She brought meaning into my life, she makes me want to live. I can't give that up, I can't give her up. So you can kill me if you like but I will die happy knowing that for once, in this marriage, I said "NO" to you.' Remi's eyes were sparks of anger.

"Then so be it, because you will die before you leave me." Akin advanced towards her.

"No! Leave her alone and face me, you bastard!" Busola was standing on shaky legs and in her hand was a knife.

"Oh, you want to kill me now?"

"Surprised? Why? You tried to kill me earlier."

"Believe me, if I wanted to, you would be dead by now. Put that knife away now!"

"No way! Remi, I want you to get out of here now and get in the car. We are leaving."

"Busola, please put the knife down. No one has to die today, please..." Remi begged. As she moved towards the door, Akin grabbed her.

"Again, my wife goes nowhere," he sneered.

"Leave me alone." Remi tried to twist herself out of his hold, but he just held on tighter. Busola moved forward but Akin used Remi has a shield against the weapon.

"Let her go!" Busola yelled.

"Drop the knife!" Akin countered.

"Never!"

"Busola, please, drop the knife. He is not worth it," Remi yelled.

Akin growled in anger and pushed Remi into a wall. He lunged at Busola and she screamed in terror because she recognised the look in his eyes. He was their father, all over again.

The knife clattered to the floor as they fought for it. Akin overpowered Busola, throwing her into the glass table in the middle of the room, then he bent down to pick up the knife. His ears deaf to the shattering of glass, he matched towards his sister.

Busola knew what would happen next. She turned to Remi who was half-conscious and watching everything with horror.

"Run, Remi, run!" She yelled with the little strength she had in her.

"No, Akin! Don't!" Remi sobbed.

But it didn't matter.

---

A YEAR LATER...

Remi shivered as the guard walked her through the gates of the state prison. She stared at the high walls with electrocuted barbed wires around the top, the stern-looking armed and uniformed men and the ferocious dogs that snarled at her. They looked ready to attack her and she prayed their leashes were held on tight.

She was led through a wide corridor with dirt-stained floors and a thick metal door that led into a high-ceilinged chamber with a table and two chairs facing each other. The room smelled terrible, like old sweat that seemed to hang on tightly to the walls. The guard motioned her to one of the iron chairs in the room.

"Wait here," he said and walked out of the room. The metal door clanged shut behind him.

"Thank you," she said to the air, trying hard not to retch. She brought out a handkerchief from her bag and spread it on the chair before she sat on it.

After a while, she heard footsteps and then the sound of keys jingling in the lock. The door swung open and the same guard walked in, accompanied by the person she had come to see.

The guard pushed the prisoner to the other chair, and with a scowl, he said, "Sit down and behave yourself. Madam, I am outside the door in case of anything."

"Okay. Thank you very much, sir," Remi said to his back as he had already turned to leave the room.

"In the case of what? Does he not know that I am your husband?" Akin was clearly irritated.

Remi looked at her husband of six years, whom she had not seen for a whole year and realised that she was truly free of him. She felt nothing for him anymore. Not even fear.

"Hello, Akin. How is prison treating you?"

"How do you think? I hate this place. I hate every single second I spend locked up in here. But don't worry, I have just a couple more years to stay here and I'm back home. We will continue with our lives, okay?" He said with authority.

"Hmmm... Really?" Remi smiled.

"Yes, yes. I never meant for things to go as far as they went that day but I'm changed and I will never hit you again. It will never happen again," he swore.

"You are right, Akin. It will never happen again because I will not come back again. I just came here to tell you that I forgive you for everything you did to me," she said calmly.

"Dammit, Remi! Stop the drama and get real! You want me to live alone in our house? How do I do that?"

"I sold the house," Remi said, staring into his eyes.

"What?!" He shrieked in disbelief.

"And your cars..."

"What the ...?"

"And your precious clothes and shoes ..."

"You did what?" He yelled.

"I sold them all, Akin, and gave part of the money to charity. I deposited some in your account for when you get out. That will help you to start your life afresh without begging anyone because people usually don't want to be associated with ex-convicts. I also kept some for myself."

"What? Remi, I swear, I will kill you when I get out, you hear me? I will." He said with quiet menace.

"Akin, I am so glad that I came. Now, I know that there is no point in looking back," she said and got up to her feet.

"Remi, you can't do this. You can't." Akin's voice broke as he tried to touch her, but the handcuffs around his wrists stopped him.

"Guard!" She yelled and the door swung open. She skirted around the table and moved quickly past her husband.

"Goodbye Akin," she whispered as she walked out of the building.

REMI STOPPED THE car beside the low-fenced cemetery and reached for the bouquet of flowers in the back seat. For the millionth time, she wished she didn't have to do this. She wished that it had never happened. She wished the flowers were fresh ones instead of plastic.

She opened the door and got out, her feet sinking into the smooth sand. She leaned against the door and shook off the sand stuck inside her flats, then walked gingerly into the cemetery.

The wind picked up dried leaves in its wake. Some danced momentarily around her ankles before returning to the call of the travelling breeze. The smell of decaying leaves assailed her nostrils as she took in the row of tombstones; some were broken, others were old with weather-worn inscriptions and some were quite new.

## Like Busola's.

She located Busola's tombstone and squatted by it. It was purple, unlike the other ones in the cemetery. Remi had chosen the colour because Busola would have loved it.

She placed the bouquet of flowers on the grave and ran her hand slowly over the headstone.

"Hi Busola," Remi said softly. She paused for a moment as if she were expecting a response from Busola.

"Hi darling, girl. How have you been? I hope you are doing well up in heaven because I know that's where you are. Well, I am fine. I am sorry I haven't been by in almost a year. I had to get back on my feet. I went to Aunty Folashade and she took care of me like you said she would. She cries for you all the time, Busola. So do I". She paused to wipe the tears from her face.

"We miss you so much. I know you are like happy and all, but it hurts. You knew who you were and what you wanted. You faced death for what you believed in. You were brave until the end and even though I wish it never happened this way, I thank you for saving my life, thank you for giving me my life back. It hurts to say it, but I am grateful, Busola. I know we shouldn't speak ill of the dead but, personally, I think you are too heady and I want you to try to tone it down up there, okay? Maybe if we had slowed it down, taken our time to execute our plan, you would still be here right now.

"I know you are not, but I am sorry you are not here anymore. You made me know what life is. You made me discover my true self. And now, I know and I will make sure that others know as well. Like you, I want to help abused women, so I got a study visa to America to take a course in mental health focusing mainly on domestic violence, sexual assault and well, general abuse. I am going to be a professional, Busola. Don't worry about the fees for I am a millionaire. I sold most of Akin's properties and disbursed the money appropriately.

"Oh, I wish you were here, we would have done this together. I would have loved to have you by my side on this exciting and fulfilling journey. But you can't be with me because you died for what you believed in. You died for my sake. He killed you. Your own brother, he killed you and would have killed me too if it wasn't for Tunde. It's because of me and I am so sorry, my sweetheart. My bossy and stubborn and kind sister. I love you so much and I will never ever forget you."

Remi cried over the headstone for a while longer. Eventually, she got to her feet, straightened her dress and walked out of there. Then she got into her car, looked over Busola's grave one last time and waved goodbye.

# 3

# WAITING ON A WISH

### *Dedication*

FOR MY DARLING SONS, JESSE, DAVID, AND DEREK; AND FOR MY DAUGHTER, ONOME WINIFRED.
FOR MY BEST FRIEND, OLOHITARE.

"Did I tell you that I passed my senior secondary school certificate exam with all A's?" Margaret shouted so loudly that Mofe could hear her over the music that was blaring from the large speakers in the spacious hall.

"You certainly did," Mofe said, nodding politely. "That's quite an achievement. Well done." His eyes scanned the room, silently praying that someone, anyone, would come and rescue him from this woman who was boring him to his very bones. She had been talking nineteen to the dozen for the past two hours and thirty-five minutes. He was actually quite amazed that anyone could talk that much in such a noisy environment.

It was their high school class reunion and it had turned out to be the total opposite of what he had envisioned it would be. He had expected it to be a quieter affair, one better suited for reminiscing about their school days and bringing each other up to date on what had happened in their lives after all those years ago. He had envisioned lots of laughter and goodwill. And to top it all off, he had envisioned that there would be cake.

Instead, there he stood, being subjected to a party so juvenile that he grimaced every time an old classmate walked up to him and said, "Great party, huh?" What seemed worse was the fact that there was no cake. You could never go wrong with cake. But there was none. Not even a slice. Or cupcakes. He always believed that there was a certain divinity to cupcakes. But nothing of the sort was anywhere in sight. That was all kinds of wrong.

And now this. This woman called Margaret who obviously seemed to know him very well had regaled him with tales of all his escapades, some of which he had since forgotten about. Yet, he could swear by one of his nuts that he had never met her before in his entire life. He had no recollection whatsoever of having ever seen or met her. She was pretty enough, so he knew that had they ever crossed paths because she would have left an impression on him. He would have recognized her otherwise.

He had already tried to escape her twice, but she was swift when it came to accosting him. And being the courteous guy that he was, he couldn't bring himself to cut her off. So he just kept listening, painfully, as she shouted every word in his face. The only blessing he saw in all this pain was the fact that her breath didn't smell bad. That was a big blessing.

He was almost at his wit's end when fortune smiled at him in the form of an angel walking across the room. Grace. She was his angel, his very best friend.

He and Grace had been friends since he was eight and she was a gap-toothed five-year-old girl. Beautiful and charming and smart, she was a crowd-puller and so popular within their circle. Everyone knew and loved her, and it sometimes got into her head, but she always quickly reverted back to being her normal self, which made her easy to like. But she was flighty and so restless, and he had always wondered what it would be like if she could just stay calm long enough for her to notice him.

She loved him alright, yes, but as a best friend. She hugged him all the time, assaulted his cheeks with kisses, teased him wickedly, and talked about everything with him, however, she still took no notice of him the way that he wanted her to. The way he saw her.

He was deeply in love with her. He had been for as long as he could remember. He would do whatever she asked of him, he wanted to make her happy every day. If only she would let him.

The problem was that she had very bad taste in men. She always fell for the losers; the shallow-minded kind who never bothered to take the time to get to know her. That's because they were never in for the long haul. They only stayed long enough to parade her around like a trophy, and then as soon as they were bored of the sex, they sprint.

He had lost count of the number of times she had cried on his shoulder after the exit of a cad. He just knew that he had thought of committing murder so many times. After each exit, he would comfort her and explain patiently to her how she was better off without any man who didn't appreciate the wonderful person that she was. He would put everything he felt into his words, hoping that she would be able to discern his undying love for her. But she would simply agree with him and promise to make a better choice in the future. Then another leather-clad hound would come by and the situation would repeat itself all over again.

The last relationship she had been in had been the worst of them all. Kayode had told everyone who cared to listen about their sexual escapades. He had even been explicit in his descriptions of what went on in the bedroom. And to top it all off, it had so happened that he was also married with two kids; something he had lied about.

Mofe had been too angry to listen to reason, so he had tailed Kayode to one of the clubs that he frequented and accosted him in the restroom. By the time he was done with him, Mofe's knuckles had hurt like hell, but it had been worth it. The sight of Kayode's bloodied mouth and nose had made it worth the hurt and bruises.

After that incident, Mofe had threatened to end his friendship with Grace if she ever got involved with the likes of Kayode and all the other wimps she seemed to get herself involved with.

Grace had promised to find a nice man to date when she was ready. The Kayode incident had sobered her, making keep to herself. The humiliation had hit her hard. And for once, the social butterfly, who once stood tall and proud with her wings spread out, hid in the shadows.

At first, he'd left her alone. But each time he looked at her, the unhappiness in her eyes killed him. So once again, he had slowly taken her through the recovery process. He took her to all the places she liked; shopping malls, karaoke bars, art galleries, the cinema, and some of their favourite restaurants. And she had begun to blossom again, to his delight. She started to live life her way again, fully and happily.

He knew he was a coward for having such intensely deep feelings for her and keeping mute about it. He just didn't want to ruin their friendship, because he knew that if he professed his love for her and she rejected him, it could harm what they shared together, and he didn't want that. So, he kept hoping that someday, she would know.

He sighed as he watched her walk into the room, her eyes scanning each face intently, looking for him. Her newly woven hair made her look younger than her twenty-eight years, and her skin was dark and shiny. She looked lush and healthy, and so beautiful. He couldn't take his eyes off of her.

And then their eyes met, and he fell in love all over again. It happened each time he looked into her eyes. Those electric and expressive eyes. He saw so much in them. He wanted to see more. He wanted to see them cloud with desire as he made passionate love to her. Wishes.

She waved at him, grinning happily. In seconds, she was beside him.

"Hi," she laughed as she hugged him.

"Hello, Grace. What took you so long?" He felt as if he had died and gone to heaven when he took in the wonderful scent of her. She smelled so damned good.

"I stopped by the bakery to get a cake. I heard there was none here, and I knew I would not hear the end of it, what with you being a cake freak and all, so I decided to go get one."

"Surely, you're an angel." Mofe gave a sigh of relief and hugged her again.

Grace laughed again. And then her eyes shifted to Margaret who was eyeing her with unguarded jealousy.

"Hi," Grace said, looking at Margaret with amusement. She was used to Mofe's girls being antagonistic towards her. They all hated her because of the closeness the two of them shared. As a matter of fact, their friendship so far had been the main cause of all Mofe's breakups. A few of them had tried to be friends with her, but it had never lasted because they couldn't understand why their boyfriend had her sitting on such a pedestal, instead of them.

"Oh, please forgive my manners," Mofe said, seeing what was going on. "Grace, this is Margaret, a friend from high school. Margaret meet Grace, my best friend."

"Hello, Grace. Hmmm, so you two are still tight, right?" Margaret didn't sound too happy about this noticeable fact.

"Like two peas in a pod," Grace ventured, smiling proudly.

This time, Margaret scowled openly at her.

"Care to dance, Mofe?" Grace said, extending her hand to Mofe who took it a little too eagerly.

"Of course," Mofe said. "Do you mind?" He looked at Margaret but did not wait for a response before being yanked away by Grace.

For the next hour, Grace and Mofe stayed close to each other, glad to be enjoying each other's company. And for that time, it began to feel more like what Mofe had expected to feel at his school's class reunion, and he gave himself to it fully. He was having fun. But he was in the middle of a sentence when he noticed Grace freeze beside him. He looked in the direction of her gaze and found himself frozen as well.

# Maxwell Promise.

He walked towards the group with the same careless swagger he had been known for in secondary school. He had grown taller since the last time Mofe had seen him, and his shoulders were broader. He was carrying a box of cake, his biceps pushing against the upper sleeves of his jacket. A neatly trimmed beard added to the physical changes that had taken place since secondary school. Mofe vaguely remembered Grace teasing him for his own lack of a beard sometime back.

He turned to look at Grace. Like everyone else, she was spellbound by the beauty of the man approaching them, walking like he owned the damn place and everybody in it. And truth be told, at that moment, he actually did own the place. And every single person in it, especially the women.

Maxwell was Grace's secondary school boyfriend. Mofe's nemesis amplified ten times over.

Grace had loved him with all her heart but he had been too much of a philanderer to stay with her. He had been the hottest guy in school, the object of admiration of many of the girls. Grace had done her best to keep him, but he had broken her heart anyway. She had been devastated for weeks, refusing to speak to anyone, even him. At first, he had tried to help her out of her misery until eventually he was forced to give up after several attempts. He had left her alone, now *his* heart broken. And the days had turned into weeks, dragging too slowly.

Eventually, she had returned to him, apologising for shutting him out. "I just needed to be on my own," she had explained. And he had pretended to understand.

Afterwards, she started to live again. However, she never spoke of Maxwell. It had scared him at first because it hadn't seemed healthy to him, but she'd seemed fine, so he let it be.

Now, Mofe watched Grace staring at Maxwell with a sinking feeling in his chest. He didn't even notice that Maxwell had reached them and was shaking hands and giving hugs.

"Grace," he called softly. She turned to look at him, a far-away look in her eyes.

"Hmmm?"

"Are you okay?"

"Oh yes, yes I am. Why; I feel wonderful," she said, a little too brightly.

"Okay. I'm here if you need anything."

"Yeah, I know. As a matter of fact, I need something. I need you to find me irresistible, Mofe. For this night only."

"What?"

"Find me irresistible. Pretend that you're crazy about me. Hold me, dance with me, be all over me, for just this one time. Please."

He looked at her and shook his head. Pretend? He *was* crazy about her. He didn't have to pretend about anything. What's going on?

"And to what end?" He knew the answer to his own question.

She didn't meet his gaze. "You know why."

Was she looking to make Maxwell jealous? He couldn't let her walk into another ditch. One look at Maxwell and Mofe could tell that he was still in the business of breaking hearts. He just knew it.

He had a better idea.

"You know, everyone is used to seeing guys fall over themselves for you but they will never get used to you in love with a guy, so I think you should find me irresistible instead. Or let's find each other irresistible."

"Hmmm. You are sharp. Real sharp. Okay, let's do it." Grace stretched out her hand to him. "Dance with me," she said softly.

"But there's no music playing right now," he said, getting out of his seat anyway.

"All the better," she smiled. He smiled back and took her in his arms and they began to move to music only they could hear.

Maxwell was staring at them. Mofe couldn't read his expression, but he knew it wasn't too friendly.

Mofe continued his dance with Grace. He pulled her closer and held her tighter. She smiled and rested her head on his shoulder.

"Is he looking?" Grace asked.

"Murderously," Mofe answered and she laughed.

"Seriously?" She asked him, raising her head to look in his face.

"Yeah. You can take a look," he offered.

"No, I don't want to. We can keep dancing," she said quickly, resting her head back on his shoulder.

*Fine by me,* he thought to himself.

He loved the feel of her hand in his, her body close to his.

He closed his eyes and rested his cheek on her head, inhaling the scent of her hair. He let his thoughts drift. To a place where there was only him, and her, and lots of water and sand and birds that fly rather than sing...

"May I?"

He was roused from his daydream by the deep baritone voice. He remembered it so well.

"What?" Mofe snapped at Maxwell.

"Cut in. May I cut in, please?" Maxwell's politeness was a facade. Mofe could tell.

"Well, I don't think so. As you can see, we are..."

"Mofe, it's okay." Grace gave him a reassuring smile.

He stared at her incredulously.

"Mo, it's fine, I promise. I'll catch up with you in a few minutes," she said.

"Sure." He nodded, flashing a fake smile of his own at Maxwell.

Maxwell was taking Grace into his arms as he moved away. High school came rushing back to him. Same script and same cast. He still had the role of the poor schmuck.

He felt anger well up within him. Anger at himself for being such a fool for love. He was angry with himself for subjecting himself time and again to this slavery. Yes, he was a slave, bound by the invisible chains of love. If only he could break those chains. If only he wanted to.

He strolled to the bar and asked for a beer, which was placed in front of him in seconds. He ignored the glass and drank straight from the bottle. Wiping his mouth with the back of his hand, he dared to steal a glance at the dancing couple a few yards away.

Maxwell was saying something to Grace. Grace threw her head back and laughed.

"Well, here we go again." He shook his head, gulped down his beer and asked for another bottle.

He was into his fourth bottle when he saw Grace walking up

to him. He saw the look in her eyes and groaned inwardly. This can't be good.

"Wow! He's completely changed, Mofe. He's brand new," she breathed excitedly.

"Yeah?" He couldn't conceal the sneer.

"Honest, he is. He said he came here for me. He's been trying to reach me for ages, Mofe. So when he was told about the reunion, he just knew it was a great opportunity to finally meet me. He said he's missed me. Can you imagine that we've both been sad and all alone all this while?"

A snort escaped from him before he could stop himself.

"Gracie, you honestly believe that Maxwell has been trying to find you for years now? A clueless and an amateur sleuth would have done a better job than this. He's lying his flying ass off, girl. I know he is."

"I know you're trying to protect me, but I'll be fine. He's asking for another chance and I'm going to give it to him," she said matter-of-factly.

"Of course!" The calm in his voice surprised him.

"What's that supposed to mean, Mofe?" She was starting to sound angry.

"Nothing. Give him a chance, you said. Okay. Do that. But I'm sorry, I can't watch another train wreck this time." He looked straight into her eyes. "Good luck to you."

She stared back for a minute and then turned on her heels and walked away. His gaze caught Maxwell's from across the room as he watched her march off. He felt his grip on the bottle tighten.

"Bartender!" he barked. "More liquor."

"By all means, Sir."

"You are a good man. A very good and kind man." Mofe smiled at him. He knew he was getting drunk, but what did it matter?

He shook his head again and looked around the hall. People were eating the cake. Cake! Cake.

He felt broken. His craving for cake was no longer there. All he wanted was to fall into a great black hole. To just keep falling and falling. More alcohol could do the trick.

His eyes scanned the room again and fell on Margaret. She was watching him so intently that he had a feeling she had willed him to look her way. He stared back at her for a while, thoughts racing through his mind.

He looked at Grace. She was laughing at something that Maxwell was saying. His arm was over her shoulder. He felt sick to the pit of his stomach.

His gaze returned to Margaret and he felt himself wave at her. She waved back. He motioned her over and in a flash, she was sitting on one of the high stools beside him.

"Hi Mofe," she breathed.

"Hey, Margaret."

Her name was really old. Well, so was Grace's. He loved Grace. Grace loved Maxwell and the other jerks. Maybe he should become a jerk.

"Are you okay?" She peered at him.

"I am. Thanks"

"I remember you used to love art back then. Do you still?" She asked.

"I sure do. As a matter of fact, I collect them now," he answered her.

"Really? That's really nice." She shuffled her seat closer. Maybe it was the alcohol or maybe he was just too distracted to notice her beauty and arresting physical attributes earlier.

He looked at Grace again and then turned to Margaret. He knew he would regret what he was about to do in two days but so what? He was tired of living life as a stumbling apology. H e took another swig of his beer. "You know, I collected some very great pieces last week. They're in my apartment right now. Would you like to see them?" His smile was slightly suggestive.

"I'd love to see them, Mofe," she purred.

"Alright then, let's go!" He got up, took hold of her hand and they started walking towards the door. At the entrance, he stopped and threw another glance at his Gracie. She was oblivious to her surroundings.

He had to move on. He was moving on.

"Shall we?" He smiled at Margaret.

"Yes," she replied.

They walked to his car. Mofe fumbled in his pockets for his car keys, and when he found them, he opened the door. He shook his head vigorously to clear the beer buzz as he turned on the ignition.

"Are you alright?" Margaret asked with concern in her voice.

He forced a smile. "Never been better."

---

GRACE TORE HER gaze from Maxwell's handsome face to look at her surroundings. She was surprised at how the crowd had thinned out. She looked at her watch and then around for Mofe but didn't see him anywhere near.

"Where's Mofe?" She turned to Maxwell.

"Dude left a while ago, babe," he replied.

"That can't be. He couldn't have left without telling me," she said.

"Well, he has left. Saw him go out with his chick."

"Mofe does not have a girlfriend," she scoffed.

"Well, he left with a girl and they seemed pretty chummy," he sneered.

"Maybe they just took a stroll. I'm sure he'll be back soon."

"I don't think so, babe. I saw them get in a car and drive off. What's with you and this Mofe dude anyway? I can't believe he still tags along with you everywhere after all these years."

"He's my best friend, Maxwell. My family. He's been there for me in everything," she spoke matter-of-factly.

"Yeah, yeah. Well, he isn't here right now and I am. Why don't you focus on me? Other chicks are dying to; you know?"

"I'm here. All my focus is on you!" She said quickly, turning to face him.

"Cool. Now, let's head to my place. I'm in the mood for something good." He winked at her.

"Er... Why don't we hold on for now? Let's concentrate on getting to know each other again before the something good? Maybe have a couple of dates?"

"Of course! Okay, no qualms at all." If he was disappointed, he succeeded in hiding it.

"Well, I should probably take you home now, right?" He said distantly, his eyes scanning the almost empty hall in the hopes of sighting one of the girls he remembered as loose. His eyes caught Erica's. She was an old fling, a stickler for him then and obviously still. She raised a hand in greeting. He nodded.

"Come on, baby, lemme get you home. I gotta head back this way again," he urged Grace, standing up.

"Okay, Max," she stood up and held her hand out to him. He took it for a moment and then released it to place his arm around her waist.

They walked out of the hall and he led her to his car, got the door open for her and settled her in. He got into his side, started the car and put on the air-conditioner.

"Damn! I think I left my glasses in there. Let me get 'em. I'll be back in a minute" he pleaded and jumped out before she could respond.

Grace watched him as he walked away, his strides long. He really was attractive and she would have loved to let him make love to her again, but she wanted some attention first. She wanted to go on a couple of dates with him; get to know the adult he had become before anything else. Mofe would be pleased to know that she finally knew how to handle herself.

Mofe! She still couldn't believe that he had left without her. Imagine him leaving with that Margaret. She knew the hawk was looking to sink her large claws into him, but it would so not work. Mofe deserved someone better, not Margaret. She knew Margaret would give her a hard time if she ended up going out with Mofe, but she told herself that nobody knew her Mofe like she did.

And that's why she didn't understand why he had left the way that he did. She vowed to call him as soon as she got home to give him a piece of her mind. What nonsense.

Meanwhile, Maxwell was in the hall talking to Erica, making arrangements for their meeting later that night. Of course, Erica was more than willing and excited to meet up with Maxwell. She remembered him as an adventurous lover. Something she could surely use now that she was bored.

Maxwell returned to the car, winked at Grace and proceeded to drive her home.

When they arrived at her place, he walked her to her door and hugged her goodnight.

"It was great seeing you again, Grace," he beamed. "You just keep getting more beautiful with time."

Grace smiled as she watched him walk away into the night. When he drove off, she locked the front door and settled in her flat and called Mofe. The phone rang and rang and rang.

---

THE NEXT MORNING, Mofe woke up with a splitting headache. He groaned in pain, and with his head in his hands, sat up. He was naked. How drunk had he been last night to not remember taking off his own clothes?

He looked up and frowned at his bedroom door. It was wide open. Then he heard a sound coming from the kitchen and got up from the bed, dragging the covers with him. The smell of freshly brewed coffee drifting in to meet his nostrils and he smiled. Just what he needed.

He went into the adjoining bathroom to take a leak and brush his teeth. He had no idea that Grace had stayed with him all night, he thought to himself as he found a pair of pants and got into them.

Grace? Had Grace followed him home last night?

He vaguely remembered the incidents of the previous night. He did remember being mad at Grace over something. Someone. Max!

He'd brought Margaret to his house and had sex with her. Great sex actually. He remembered how incredible her body had looked, how smooth her skin had felt. Her small, perky breasts had been so sensitive. Her fresh breath and her moans of pleasure had taken him overboard.

He made his way towards the kitchen where the smell of coffee was wafting stronger. He walked in and stopped.

Margaret was making breakfast in his kitchen, naked. Suddenly, everything came back to him. Last night. Margaret. Grace. Maxwell. The beer buzz. The sex.

He couldn't take his eyes off the gorgeousness that was Margaret's body. He felt a rush of blood flood to his head.

"Good morning, Margaret," he said quietly.

"Oh, good morning, darling. I'm sorry for invading your kitchen, but I figured you would need some food this morning to regain your strength if you know what I mean." She smiled knowingly, pushing a tiny tray of steaming coffee before him.

"Thanks a lot," he said, smiling at her. Then he took a sip of his coffee. "Hmmm, it tastes good. Thanks," he said.

"You're welcome. Now sit down and have some toast." She pulled out a chair for him and he sat down obediently.

He watched her movements as she served him breakfast. He couldn't keep his eyes off of her. How could he? She was still very naked and so brazen about it. She had great confidence in her body and justifiably so, she was hotter than hell.

She filled a mug for herself and sat down across him, her legs slightly parted. He told himself he wouldn't look there.

He looked there.

They made love all day long. They only surfaced at noon to have lunch, then went back to bed.

"Goodness, woman, you will be the death of me," Mofe said breathlessly.

"Not if you beat me to it," she countered, a silly smile playing on her lips.

"It's a good thing it's Saturday. What would we have done about work?" Mofe asked.

"Well, I hardly ever call in sick, so..." She laughed and he joined her.

His mind strayed to Grace for the umpteenth time. He still felt bad about leaving the party without telling her. She had been so engrossed in that slimy bastard, Maxwell, that he didn't want to go there and make a fool of himself again.

He knew she would be upset with him by now, or maybe not. For the first time, he didn't care too much. Margaret was worth the trouble that Grace was going to give him later. Besides, she would be with her precious Maxwell right now, just as he was with Margaret, so there was really no sense in stressing about anything.

"You're far away. Where in the world are you?" Margaret teased him.

"I was just thinking of what to do about dinner. I'm very hungry." He answered.

"Yeah, me too. I could make us something," she offered.

"No, let's go out to eat. I don't want to stress you."

"It's no stress, darling."

"Margaret, I'm asking for a date here. Please, don't make me beg for it."

"Really? Oh wow! It's different with you for sure. Usually, it's a date before sex but with you, it's sex and then a date. That's great!" She laughed.

She was right. Some guys would not even bother taking the next step after having what many consider "free" sex with a woman. But she deserved it. She was beautiful, she genuinely liked him, and she took his mind off Grace. She deserved to be treated with the utmost respect and he would do just that.

So they showered and went out to eat. And afterwards, they went to a nice lounge where he was one of the patrons, to have some drinks and talk.

They had been there for about two hours when Grace and Maxwell walked in. He felt the jolt before he even saw her. It had always been that way. He swore under his breath.

"What is it?" Margaret asked.

"Oh, nothing. Grace just walked in," he explained. Margret's face tightened with displeasure. He waved at Grace, who had already seen him and was staring at him with daggers in her eyes and nodded at Maxwell.

"And she's going to be a little spoilsport as usual, right?" Margaret was scowling.

"What do you mean?"

"You know what I mean. She's always causing issues between you and your girlfriends. She determines who stays or goes. You always choose her over other girls and I'm still surprised that you two have nothing with each other."

"That's not true, Margaret. I left the other girls because they had one issue or another and Grace just happened to help by pointing them out to me," he argued.

"Oh really? Just as she would point mine out to you, right? So, what will it be? I talk too much? That I hopped into bed with you the first night? Or the fact that she just doesn't like me?"

"See here, Margaret, don't ruin this magical time for us, please. As a matter of fact, let's leave, please." He said, standing up. She was only too glad to follow suit.

They stopped briefly by Grace's table to say hello and then they walked out. They were almost pulling out when Mofe saw Grace walking briskly towards them as she flagged him down.

"Here we go," Margaret hissed.

"It's nothing," Mofe said, as he excused himself.

Grace looked lovely in a short black jacket over a red jumpsuit and white sandals.

"Mofe, I can't believe that you left me at the reunion yesterday. As if that wasn't enough, you left with talkative Margaret and didn't even bother to call me or return my calls. I called you God knows how many times and you didn't even think to call me back." Grace always looked out of breath when angry.

"I'm sorry, Grace. And please, don't call her that," he said quietly.

"Call her what? Isn't that what we called her yesterday?" She looked shocked.

"That was yesterday, Grace. A lot has happened since yesterday." He replied with a smile.

"A lot has happened? What could have happened? Did she bewitch you or something?" She asked and he smiled again.

"Are you done? I need to get back to my date and I'm sure yours is waiting for you as well," he stated.

"I don't care. Let her wait. I'm not done talking."

"Gracie, I'm really sorry that I left the party last night without telling you. I didn't want to disturb you. "

"Hmmm"

"I have to go, Grace. I'll give you a call, okay?" And with that, he turned and walked back to the car and drove off.

When he looked into the rear-view mirror as the car moved away, his heart melted. Grace was standing there staring at him. She looked so alone. Well, good for her. She was the one losing her head over that snake, Maxwell.

Grace walked back into the lounge with slow and unhappy strides. She felt like she was losing her best friend and the feeling hurt. She wanted to go home, lie down and cry alone. She didn't have it in her to make small talk with Maxwell and ward off his advances at the same time. When she got to their table, she sat down.

"So, dude finally grew a spine and found himself a chick, huh?" Maxwell scoffed.

"What do you mean?" She asked.

"Your friend, Mofe. He's been so in love with you that he couldn't keep a chick. But he seems to have fallen out of love with you now." he said.

"He's been so in love with me? He's fallen out of love with me? What are you saying? Mofe has never been in love with me. He just loves me as a friend," she said, surprised.

"Ask everyone. He's so in love with you, just like a little puppy. You really are one naïve girl, you know. Well, it works for me." He laughed.

"What? Mofe has been in love with me?" She whispered, looking into the distance.

"That's right. Anyway, where were we?"

"Max, can we please leave? I don't feel too well." Her voice shook.

"What? I had tonight all planned out. Why are you such a killjoy?" He looked upset.

"I'm sorry. I'll make it up to you. Just take me home, please," she pleaded.

And, grumbling all the way, he did.

She waited until he drove off and then she dashed out, got into her car and sped off to Mofe's place.

---

"THANK YOU, MOFE." Margaret's soft whisper roused him from his thoughts.

"Hmmm? What are you thanking me for?" He quizzed. They were lying on the sofa in the sitting room watching TV. He pulled her closer to him, her body so soft against his.

"For standing up for me tonight."

'Standing up for you?' He looked confused.

"Yeah, with Grace earlier this evening."

"Whoa! How do you know about that?"

"I have perfect hearing."

"That is called eavesdropping, Marge."

"Darling, I was just looking out for me. I was a little apprehensive because that girl seems to have such a strong hold on you. I just wanted to know what you two were arguing about, that's all. And I'm happy I did because you made me feel really good. However, I'm sorry for eavesdropping."

"That was really naughty of you." He shook his head.

"Again, I'm sorry."

"Hmmm. How sorry are you?" He asked as he bent down his head to nibble on her neck.

"Very, very sorry" she whispered, her voice dropping to an almost slur.

"Hmmm," he said and turned her to face him, then he kissed her...

---

GRACE STOOD BY Mofe's window unable to tear her eyes away. Disgust surged through her as she watched Margaret writhe on the sofa, her face contorted in lines of pleasure.

She felt sick to her stomach. It was hard to believe what Maxwell had said now that she was here and watching Mofe and Margaret.

If Mofe was truly in love with her then why was he touching and kissing another woman so lovingly? He had only met her yesterday. How come they looked so intimate? She felt like she was missing something.

*"Is this the same guy who is supposedly in love with me?"* She asked no one in particular.

She felt pain deep in her heart as she watched Margaret take off her top. It was a pain she couldn't understand. And a moment later, Mofe got up, took Margaret by the hand and they hurried to the bedroom, giggling all the way there.

She wanted to bang on the door and throw a spanner into the works. She wanted so bad to see the look on Margaret's face when she saw her standing there; spoilsport Grace.

Instead, she turned around and went back to her car; where she sat for a long time, her mind tortured by the image of Mofe and Margaret having sex. She knew they were having sex. The lights were out in the bedroom, what else could they possibly be doing?

He was probably already in love with Margaret.

She felt like dying. Her body started to tremble. She rested her head on the wheel and let the tears come.

---

LYING AWAKE UNDER the covers, Mofe scrolled through his missed calls. There were twenty-five of them from Grace. He had said he would call. He wanted to call her but it was too late to do so. It was two in the morning and every normal person would be asleep by now.

Still ... he decided to text her.

Awake?

She was tempted to ignore his message, but she wanted to talk to him so badly. So she answered him in the affirmative.

How are you doing? Are you home? He sent another one.

I'm okay. Yes, I'm home. Where else would I be?

You could be at Max's.

Well, I'm not.

Apparently. How come you're not asleep?

Got stuff on my mind. How come you aren't?

Margaret was fast asleep beside him but he wasn't. He couldn't find sleep, so he needed a distraction. Oh, who was he kidding? He needed to speak with his Grace.

Got stuff too. Can I call you so we can talk about it?'

Okay.

He slid gently out of bed so he wouldn't rouse Margaret, and tiptoed out of the room. He went to the kitchen to get a soda and strolled into the sitting room and flopped down on the sofa. He stretched his full length on the sofa and then he called her.

They talked for hours, just like old times. They filled each other in on the events of the past two days. She was careful not to let him hear the pain in her voice when he spoke about Margaret. He said nice things about her, saying he wanted to give their relationship a chance. He was serious with Margaret. He said he liked her.

Her heart ached as she said things to him that she didn't mean. She was not happy for him, but she lied and said that she was. She told him that Maxwell was wonderful, which was also a lie.

She had no chance with Mofe. He liked Margaret.

Mofe felt a knife slice through his heart when Grace spoke glowingly of Maxwell. He couldn't believe how clueless she was. Max was a jerk, a first-class jerk. How come she was so blind to all of that? It was a good thing that he had Margaret to distract him from the anger that flooded him when he thought about her with Maxwell.

He realized once again that he had no chance with Grace. She was still into jerks. A good guy like himself would never do.

He decided to change the subject to a lighter one and she went along with the flow. They continued talking until she drifted off to sleep.

And that was how Margaret found him the next morning.

The days turned into weeks and the weeks turned into months. Margaret and Mofe became a well-known couple in their circle. Everyone knew them as the power couple. Mofe took her to meet his mother and the two women bonded well.

Grace, on the other hand, had decided to end things with Maxwell because she had realised that he wasn't the kind of man she needed. Her eyes had finally opened up and now, with that realisation came pain as she realized how much time she had wasted on his type. She knew better now, wanted better. But the "better" she suddenly found herself craving for, now belonged to someone else.

Not too long ago, he was simply Mofe to her; a boy she had grown up with, one who had stuck closer than a brother. But now, he was this great guy she couldn't have.

She had thought about coming clean with him a couple of times, but his closeness to Margaret looked so real that she decided to let it be. Let him be happy without her. He deserved it.

Margaret was a high-powered and energetic career woman. And she, Grace, was a mere artist. It had gotten to a point where she was tempted to throw her easel, canvas, and painting brushes into the dumpster, and pursue a career just like Margaret. She had even sent out her resume to a couple of companies and received several calls to be interviewed, but, each time, she had backed out at the last minute. Because she knew deep within her that being a corporate chick was not for her. She would just end up being as miserable as she had been with Maxwell.

Mofe had it easier than Grace did. He had Margaret. She was very devoted to him and to their relationship. She spoiled Mofe silly. She made him all kinds of meals. She even employed a housekeeper who kept his flat tidy. She initiated romantic dinners and getaways. It was a pretty picture and everyone envied Mofe, but they were also happy for him because the heavens had finally smiled on him.

He liked Margaret a lot, but deep down, he knew that he didn't love her. At least not the way that he knew he should. He could spend the rest of his life with her, but he would never feel for her the way he felt for Grace.

Grace touched his innards. She was seated inside of him and there was no way to get her out. He didn't know how he had survived the past six months without being with her and he missed her every single day.

They spoke on the phone occasionally and the few times that they did, he would close his eyes and let her sweet voice wash over him. What he felt for Margaret was nothing compared to what he felt for Grace. She was his being and he hurt every day and pined piteously for her.

One evening, he decided to go to one of the galleries he frequented to source for new works, and on display was one of her latest paintings. It was one of a half-naked woman sitting on a beach, staring unseeingly at the distant, outgoing ship. She was wet from the rain that fell on her and one hand was stretched towards the ship.

His breath caught in his throat as he saw the deep sadness depicted in the painting. He couldn't keep his eyes off of it, so he knew that he had to get it for himself. He did just that and headed home, his heart beating hard in his chest.

Grace was sad. Troubled. She was crying every time. That stupid jerk had hurt her again. He knew it. He had been too busy with Margaret to notice.

He felt like kicking himself for being so callous to Grace. It was his job to look after her. He wasn't a bad person. He took care of people who meant squat to him, yet he had neglected the one person who meant the entire world to him. He felt terrible as he drove into his compound and got out of the car, his precious painting under his arm as he hurried inside.

It was a good thing that Margaret had a presentation at work the next day. It had forced her to stay away from his place, leaving him with time alone, and happily so. He could study the painting with a clear mind.

Once inside his flat, he headed straight to his study and switched on the lights and hung the painting on the wall. Then he studied it for a very long time until he felt the wetness on his cheeks. He wiped his tears with the back of his hand and took out his phone.

She answered on the third ring. Her 'hello' was soft, and so was his.

"Grace..."

"Yes, Mofe..."

"Are you okay?"

*No, I'm not, you idiot! I miss you with all that I am.*

"I am, thanks," she answered instead.

*Then why are you so sad? I can feel your sadness inside of me. It's tearing me apart. Tell me what's wrong with you and I'll fix it.*

"You are?"

*Of course not, you moron. I wish you were here with me. I wish we were together. I'm dying without you.*

"Mofe, I'm fine. And you?"

*Me? I'm dead without you. I'm walking, I'm eating, I'm working, I'm laughing and I'm having tons of sex, but I'm dead, okay?*

"Yeah, I'm alright. I just thought to call ... you know, check up on you."

*You should do more than just call to check on me, Mofe. You should come and see me.*

"That's kind of you. Thank you."

*What are you thanking me for? I've failed you miserably. I don't deserve your thanks.*

"It's nothing. How was your day?" Mofe asked her.

*Long and miserable because you're not with me.*

"It was great, thank you. Tell me you had a great day..."

*How possible is it to have a great day without you? All of my days without you have been worthless.*

"Yeah, I did. I did."

*Of course, you did. With you and Margaret ravaging each other every chance you get, of course, you would have a great day.*

"Okay. And Margaret?"

"Margaret is fine. She's fine. And Max?"

*Of course, Margaret is fine! She works out. She eats healthy. She has you. She would be fine, the toughie!*

"Good. Maxwell's great, thanks."

"Grace...?"

"Yes?"

Silence. They listened to the sound of each other's breathing.

"Goodnight, Grace."

"Goodnight, Mofe."

He ended the call and pulled out a chair and sat down. The heaviness in his heart made his breath come in gulps.

"Hmmm, this is new. Who's the artist?" Margaret asked as she stood, studying the painting in Mofe's study.

"A good friend of mine," Mofe answered, guardedly. He was sitting behind his desk working on his computer.

"Yeah? Which of them?"

"Grace."

"Grace? Did you buy her painting? Where? When?" She asked, looking at him and then back at the painting.

"Looks like so. I got it yesterday, at Oasis Gallery," he responded.

"Why did you buy it?"

"Why? Well, I saw it and I liked it."

"You like this? I don't see why you like it. It's... it's disturbing. I don't like it at all."

"Well, I do," he smiled at her.

She went back to studying the painting for a few more minutes and then she asked, "Was she there?"

"What? Who?"

"Grace. Did you see her? Did you speak with her?"

"No."

"So, you just saw the painting by chance and bought it immediately? And you didn't think to ask me first?"

"Ask you first? Am I required to ask you before investing in my business? I buy paintings all the time and you've never asked me this question before, so why now?"

"Because it's Grace! Everywhere I look, I see Grace. I see her written all over your face. You always mention her in our conversations, whether it's about her or not. You jump to her defence all the time. You're always ready to help her out and rescue her from trouble. Frankly, I'm tired of having her in my face all the time."

"Margaret," Mofe said, his voice surprisingly calm. "Grace is my friend."

"So what? You think I don't have friends? Do I throw them in your face like you throw her in mine?" Margaret was obviously angry.

"Margaret, you are taking this too seriously. You need to calm down."

"I will calm down only when you make a choice between her and me." She spat vehemently.

He was taken aback. A surprised laugh escaped him. "Don't do this, Margaret. Don't, please."

"Are you mocking me?"

"I would never do that, Margaret. Just be calm and let me explain something to you, okay? Please, take a seat." He offered.

"I'm all ears," she huffed as she flopped on an extra chair and folded her arms across her chest.

Mofe sighed deeply and began.

"My father died when I was just 7 years old. My mother couldn't bear the pain of living in our house without him so a year later, she took me and we moved from Ibadan to Lagos. We got a two-bedroom flat at Ikotun because funds were really low and we had no one to help us. My mother got a job as a nurse at a nearby hospital and her salary took good care of us.

"We had some neighbours then, Mr and Mrs Adedeji, and they had a five-year-old daughter named Bisi. She was their only child. Her parents were financially better off than us. They had a car, their apartment was far nicer than ours, but they weren't happy. They quarrelled all the time, and Bisi took to running to our flat whenever these fights started. My mother would comfort her and tell us stories to distract her.

"It became a constant occurrence as the fights increased. They were so involved in their quarrels that they totally neglected the poor girl. At first, she was really morose, but my mother and I showed her so much affection that she blossomed and became happy again. We lived this way for two whole years.

"Then, one night, her father got killed in a car crash..."

"Oh no!" Margaret exclaimed.

"Yes. He had been heavily drunk. Her mother went berserk. She locked herself in her room and cried for days. She forgot all about her little daughter but thank God we were there. My mother took very good care of her and made sure that she had all she needed. My mother also tried to reach out to Mrs Adedeji to no avail. She rejected all the offers my mother extended to her, so we left her well alone and concentrated on Bisi instead. My mother explained what had happened to the little girl and she seemed to take it well. My mother ensured that she lacked nothing at all and the girl continued to glow.

"A month later, Mrs Adedeji staggered into our apartment unannounced. She was looking thin and dishevelled, and she reeked of alcohol. She asked for her daughter, and against my mother's better judgment, she released Bisi to her. The little girl looked sad as her mother dragged her away and I felt pain in my heart as I watched her go. But my mother hugged me tight and assured me she would return.

"My mother waited for two days - which had seemed like an eternity to me - and went to their flat to check on them, but Mrs Adedeji didn't allow her in. She just answered her from the window and assured her that all was well. She saw Bisi through the window, sitting demurely in the living room and staring into space. She decided to let them be as they needed time to mourn the late Mr Adedeji.

"The days went by fast and a week later, my mother returned home from work one day looking worried. I asked her what the problem was and she told me everything was fine. But she went out again and called other neighbours. They all stood in front of the Adedeji's flat and muttered amongst themselves. I noticed that they were covering their noses.

"My mother began to yell Bisi's name but there was no answer. I saw panic fill her face as she ordered the men to break down the door. They did without much effort.

"A moment later, my mother came out of the house bearing a frail looking Bisi in her arms. Mrs Adedeji had locked herself and her daughter up in her room and drank poison. Her daughter had watched her die and the shock had rendered her immobile for days.

"Oh my God," Margaret whispered.

"It took a lot to bring Bisi out of that state, but we succeeded. She became happy again. No family member came to claim her, so my mother adopted her and renamed her Grace because she said it was the grace of God that had kept her. And we grew up together, from that time up till now, Margaret. So you should understand that I can't just break away from her like that. My mother would be deeply upset because it would seem like I'm disowning my own blood. So please, for my sake, try to get along with her. You don't have to visit her or call her or even speak with her. Just have an open mind about her. Don't be so antagonistic towards her, please."

"I know. Oh my God. I'm so sorry for my behaviour. I had no idea. Oh, poor girl. I wish there was something I could do for her." Margaret moved into his arms and held on tightly.

"Just accept her, Margaret. That's all I need," he whispered, as he held her back.

"Okay, I will. I have," she laughed, wiping her eyes.

"Thank you," he said; his face lighting up. Then he kissed her.

"You are so welcome, baby."

The following weekend, Margaret invited Grace over for dinner. Grace felt awkward about going. She expressed as much to Mofe when he called to tell her.

"Mofe, I don't think I want to come. I don't know Margaret that well. I think she's a manipulative person. She doesn't want you hanging out with me anymore, why would she just invite me for dinner out of the blue?"

"Come on, Grace! Relax. Margaret is a nice person once you get to know her and she doesn't hate you. You need to try to get along with her because she's my woman. See, she hasn't done anything wrong here, Grace. She's just a girl who met a guy and fell in love with him, that's all. Please try, for my sake? Please?" Mofe had pleaded.

His words hurt her more than he would ever know. It made her want to argue some more, but she knew she had no genuine reason to decline Margaret's invitation. Besides, it was her chance to spend some time with him also, so she sighed and agreed to show up. She couldn't explain how much she'd missed him. She should have let him know how she felt about him a long time ago.

If only he hadn't always acted like a big brother to her; demanding to know her whereabouts all the time, scaring off potential boyfriends he suspected were no good for her, and beating up the ones who did, things might have been different and she would have known how he felt about her. Instead, he had put on this brother façade that masked any romantic feelings he may have had for her.

Now she had to go and have dinner with the love of her life and his 'woman', a woman she couldn't stand. She had to pretend she was happy for them. She wanted them to break up and never make up. That would really make her happy.

She sighed as she opened her closet again. She had changed clothes five times already. None of her dresses seemed to fit. They were all out of shape today. She needed a change of wardrobe.

She knew she was just kidding herself. She wanted to look spectacular for Mofe and none of the dresses in there were good enough. She would just stop by a boutique and get a new dress.

She would get through dinner. All she needed to do was to look nice.

MOFE WAS NERVOUS about Grace's visit, but he did his best to hide it from Margaret. She was a smart girl, so he was a bit anxious that she might be able to pick up on it anyway. Also, he didn't want Grace to find out that he had told Margaret her story. He prayed Margaret would not let any of it out, although he had warned her not to mention anything to Grace.

He was nervous and at the same time excited. He hadn't seen Grace in a long time and he was just dying to behold her beautiful face again.

He needed to look his best. Perhaps, she would find him attractive for once.

"Yeah, right," he snorted to himself.

He decided he was going to look his best all the same. That would not hurt anyone. But did he have his best in his closet? To be on the safe side he would just stop over at a friend's boutique and pick up a nice shirt; probably a pair of pants to go with it. Also, there was this really great Italian shoe he'd seen there one time; he would just add that to the cart. And why not a bottle of good cologne to go with everything? That would do.

Dinner would have been an awkward affair if Margaret hadn't been so great at being a hostess. She had organized countless parties before so it was a piece of cake for her. Conversation flowed freely because she was a talker and she knew quite a lot.

She smiled and talked, and paid attention to every detail. Grace felt herself beginning to relax after a while and she started to really enjoy herself. She even laughed at Margaret's stories.

Mofe looked so good in a leaf-green, short-sleeved shirt. She caught her breath each time she looked at him. She ached with longing for him. She recalled all the times that they'd hugged each other as friends and she wished they could go back to those times. Everything had been so simple back then, now it had become one big, complicated affair.

Mofe wondered how he would have coped with being near Grace without touching her if Margaret hadn't been so in charge of everything. She was the most beautiful woman he knew. She was wearing a white, knee-length dress that clung to her body like a second skin. Margaret had sat them side by side, making him swallow each time her arm brushed his. The room felt hot and he yearned to go outside for some fresh air.

After dinner, Margaret ushered them out to the balcony so that she could clear the table. Grace offered to help her, but Margaret had waved her off.

"You are our guest so you shouldn't lift a finger. Besides, I love cleaning up after the party, so go along, Grace," she smiled.

And that's how Grace and Mofe had ended up sitting side by side in the twin chairs on the balcony, staring up at the sky. It was a full moon, and the stars twinkled across the dark bed.

"You look very beautiful tonight, Grace," Mofe murmured, looking at her, taking in all of her loveliness.

"Thank you for noticing. You look incredibly handsome yourself. Margaret is one lucky girl." She smiled.

'Hmmm. I think I'm the lucky one here. She's great!"

"She is. You were right; she is nice."

"Yeah," he smiled wryly.

"So you told her, right?" Grace smiled at him.

"Told her what?" He seemed lost.

"Stop it, Mofe. You told Margaret my story. I saw it in her eyes and actions. It was too obvious."

"Oh, drats! Yes, I did. I just wanted her to understand our closeness. Are you mad?"

"I'm not. But I understand now that you are serious about her."

"Hmmm"

## HARD ROCK. SCISSORS. HE WAS IN THE MIDDLE.

"Look, Mofe, a shooting star!" Grace pointed excitedly at the star that shot rapidly across the sky.

"Where?" he sat up.

"There. Oh, quick, make a wish!" she exclaimed as she quickly shut her eyes and muttered something. She opened her eyes to find him doing the same thing.

"What did you wish for?" she asked softly.

"Something I've wanted all my adult life," he replied, gazing into her eyes intensely.

"Really? Me too." She smiled at him. "Do you believe our wishes could come true?"

"Maybe. If mine came true, I would gladly die afterwards."

"Yeah? I think I would also," she said, nodding as she looked at him and wondered if he truly was once in love with her.

She felt herself shivering as they kept looking into each other's eyes. She ached with need for him and she felt a sudden urge to tell him so.

Mofe felt ready to pull Grace close to him and kiss her lovely lips. His eyes settled on them and he began to dream of how wonderfully soft they would feel against his.

Grace felt her breath get caught in her throat as Mofe feasted his eyes on her lips. His eyes were raw with longing. He did love her! She needed to tell him that she cared for him as well.

"Mofe…" she whispered.

"Yes, Grace…" he said huskily, leaning into her.

"Wow! What a beautiful sky!" Margaret's voice sliced through the thick magic that hung around the balcony and Grace jumped back.

"It is, right?" Mofe straightened up too.

"Yes, it's so romantic." She moved past Grace and went to sit in Mofe's lap.

Grace groaned inwardly.

"I have to use the bathroom," she said, excusing herself and walking off briskly to the bathroom. Once there, she turned on the tap, bent her head and splashed cold water on her face. Then she straightened up and looked at herself in the mirror. Her eyes were dazed. She looked drunk and ravaged.

"Oh my God!" she whispered. She barely recognized the person staring back at her.

He did feel something for her. She had felt it, she had seen it. How could she ignore that now?

*I need to get out of here,* she thought to herself as she wiped her face with toilet paper. After she had re-applied her make-up, she stepped out of the bathroom.

"Hey guys, I have to leave now," she called out to them from the sitting room and they both came in to meet her.

"So soon? Why?" Mofe asked her with a frown.

"I have a meeting in the morning and I need to go and prepare for it. It's quite late and I really need to go," she cringed inwardly at her lie, avoiding eye contact with Mofe. She did not want to embarrass herself any further by making her feelings known.

"You've done more than enough just by coming, Grace. Thank you." Margaret smiled.

"Thanks so much for dinner, Margaret. It was lovely. I'll return this kindness soon. Thanks again."

"'The pleasure was ours, babes. Let's see you off."

And she led the way out.

---

"Mama, I told Margaret that you adopted Grace," Mofe said to his mother as they stood in her kitchen. He had decided to pay her a long overdue visit.

"Young man, I did not raise you to be a liar." She looked at him with a serious glint in her eyes and handed him a soda. The grey tints in her soft afro gave her a distinguished look. She was still very vibrant, despite her old age and she moved around with ease.

"I know, Mama. I just needed her to get off Grace's case," he said, as he followed her into the sitting room.

"Hmmm… what else did you lie about, oko mi?" She smiled at her grown son who had been just a little boy a little while ago. She settled herself in the double-seater, and he sat beside her, cradling his drink in his hands.

"Nothing else, Mama. I just told her you adopted Grace."

"Well, in a way, I did."

"Yeah, but not legally. She thinks of Grace as my sister now. All her annoyance is gone."

"You don't sound too happy about that," his mother observed.

"You know me too well, Mami. I just wanted to get Margaret to accept Grace not to be close with her. Last weekend she insisted on having Grace over for dinner. And just last night she was talking about the two of them going shopping together. Sort of like a sister-in-law thing. I really am not comfortable with it."

"Well, my son, acceptance comes with a lot of things. Accepting someone means sharing your life with that person, giving to that person and just being there for them. So, Margaret has not done anything wrong here."

"Yes, I know, Mama."

"Grace isn't your sister. I didn't raise you two as brother and sister. I just told you to always look out for her, considering all that she had gone through. You could have told her that, Mofe, but you didn't because you are guilty of being in love with Grace and you were afraid that Margaret would realize that fact."

"Yeah." He looked at his hands like they had blood on them.

"My son, you seem confused right now, but I trust you to always do the right thing. You are just like your father, a wonderful man even in death. So, what are you going to do?"

"I want to propose to Margaret, Mama. It's about time," Mofe announced.

"Hmmm... And Grace?" She raised one eyebrow.

"Grace doesn't love me. Not in the way that I want her to, so I've decided to move on. Margaret is a great girl and I love her in my own way. She's not a terrible person to live with, so I'm sure it will work out.'

"Okay, oko mi. I like Margaret; she's steady, very efficient and hardworking. If she is really your choice, then you have my blessing."

"Yes Ma, I've made up my mind about that." He sounded firm. His mother looked at him and smiled.

"My son is getting married."

"Yes, Mama, I am." Mofe smiled back at her. He felt relieved. He was happy that his mother was happy.

"That's wonderful, my husband. Please, excuse me." She got up and went into her bedroom. When she returned a few minutes later, she was holding a small jewellery box in her hand. She held it out to Mofe.

"Maami, are you proposing to me?" He asked in mock surprise and she laughed heartily.

"Haba! You have been my husband for years now. Open the box," she urged him gently.

He did. Inside the box lay a beautiful engagement ring.

"Wow," he said almost breathlessly. "It's lovely, Mama, but I already got a ring."

"Your father gave it to me and I wanted you to give it to Grace."

At that, Mofe looked up sharply.

"Yes," his mother continued. "I had always hoped that the two of you would grow up and get married, but you've been too afraid to tell her that you love her, and she in turn…"

"She, in turn, what, Mama?"

"Well, we don't know if she could love you too. You never even tried to find out, Mofe. What are you so afraid of?"

"At dinner the other night, Grace and I were out on the balcony and we had a shooting star experience. She urged me to make a wish and I did. I wished that she would love me and Mama for about a moment afterwards, it felt like she did. She had this look in her eyes that shook me to my core. I could have said something to her that night if Margaret hadn't walked in. I guess wishes last for just a moment," he said, smiling wryly.

"No, they don't. Wishes last for as long as you want them to. Whatever you wish for in your heart comes to pass for you, and as long as you continue to genuinely desire that thing it will always remain with you. Why don't you wait it out a little bit? Postpone the proposal for now and see if your wish will come true. Unless you really want to get married to Margaret. You have my blessing in whatever you choose to do."

"Thank you, Mama." He looked at her and smiled.

"You are welcome, my husband," she said as she hugged him.

After leaving his mother, Mofe went to the beach. He needed some place peaceful where he could think. He took off his shoes and started to stroll in the sand.

Margaret was very intelligent and good at her job. She was a leader, serious-minded, with a drive that was infectious. She knew what she wanted and she went for it. She was independent and self-sufficient. A tough woman. She was also beautiful and sexy. With Margaret, he had to be on his toes.

Grace, on the other hand, was soft and vulnerable. She preferred to be led by her man. She was a great artist; her works were always vivid and stirring. She was funny and playful and mischievous. She had a huge heart, which earned her different categories of friends.

Once, she had cancelled a date with him because she wanted to attend a friend's daughter's wedding. He had later found out that this supposed friend happened to be the security guard who worked in her building.

Grace was homely and sweet. She was also emotional and forgiving and took life easy. With her, he felt restful. He could be with her in one spot for one whole year without missing anyone or anything else. Grace was his last bus stop. She was the missing part of him.

He liked Margaret because of the things she did for him, but he loved Grace for no reason. She was just the love of his life.

He was steady like Margaret; they had so much in common. He was career-driven as well, a leader to the core. But in his relationship with Margaret, he seemed to have left the reins to her. He just let her handle everything, and so far, she had done extremely well. He could find no fault with her. None at all. He had no reason not to marry her.

Several hours later, he drove away from the beach. His decision was made. The road to Grace seemed too far. He put on some music and continued on his journey.

When he got to her place he saw that the blinds were shut, and the whole place was in total darkness.

"Oh drats!" He kicked himself for not calling her first. He dialled her number and she answered after two rings.

Then he saw the living room lights come on. A few seconds later, the front door opened and she came out to meet him.

"What are you doing here?" She smiled pleasantly. She couldn't hide the fact that she was very glad to see him.

"What? You aren't happy to see me?" He teased her as he hugged her.

"Of course, I am. Come on in." She ushered him inside the house and locked the door behind them.

"Hmmm. I've missed this place," he smiled, taking in the

cosy living room. There were just two seats, a long sofa in the middle of the room and a wide loveseat with a lamp beside it in one corner. The walls were in muted yellow and the drapes in warm honey.

The ambience of the room was warm, serene and beautiful.

He felt relaxed and peaceful here.

The room. The woman. Everything held such great appeal for him.

"The place has missed you too!" Grace said. She was watching Mofe, wondering what had brought him to her house.

"Then it's a happy reunion," he said, and they both laughed.

"Come and sit beside me," he said, patting the seat as he himself lowered his frame into the sofa.

"Em, I could, but then I would burn dinner. I'll be right back." She patted him on the head and ran off into the kitchen.

She was excited. So very excited. Her man had come visiting at last. She was going to make this visit so memorable that he would want to return over and over again.

Meanwhile, Margaret dialled Mofe's number for the umpteenth time without getting a response. It had been hours since his mother had told her that he had left her place. She was worried to her bone, imagining all sort of gruesome pictures. She even said a silent prayer for him.

After Grace had set the table for dinner, she went into the living room to get Mofe only to find him fast asleep on the sofa. She squatted beside him wondering whether to wake him up. He looked so peaceful. She decided to let him sleep.

Then she sat on the floor, facing him and took in his handsome features. She desired to kiss him, just lightly. Not enough to wake him up but enough to make him have sweet dreams. Instead, she just sat there staring at him. After a while, his eyelids began to move. She started to get up, but it was too late, his eyes flew open and he saw her sitting there.

"I knew it!" he murmured, stretching.

"Knew what?"

"That you were staring at me, willing me to wake up."

At that point, the natural thing to do would have been to go into his arms and kiss him senseless. But she couldn't. Because he wasn't hers to kiss. He was forbidden. Taboo. She felt the lump in her throat.

She couldn't speak, so she grabbed his arm and pulled him up and led him to dinner.

After dinner, they went back to the sitting room and just talked. They talked until Mofe glanced at his watch and winced at how late it was. It was ten at night.

"You have to go? I wish you didn't have to go," Grace said sadly.

"Me too, Gracie," he said and hugged her to him.

"Will you visit again?" She sounded like a child, and he just wanted to please her every day.

"A million watchdogs couldn't keep me away," he scowled playfully.

"Okay. That's comforting," she smiled.

"You'll be fine, right?" He looked concerned.

*Not without you, no.*

"Yes," she said, trying to sound confident.

"Good. There's something I want to ask you, Gracie." And this time, he was not faking his seriousness.

"What?" Grace asked expectantly.

He took a deep breath before looking into her eyes.

"I'm going to ask Margaret to marry me. What do you think?"

Grace heard loud drumming in her ears. Mofe was saying something but the drumming prevented her from hearing him. She couldn't read his lips because her vision was blurred. She felt wetness on her cheeks and realized she was crying.

"Gracie, you are crying…" And from his heart sprouted hope. She was sad that he was getting married. That's the reaction he had hoped for.

"Yes, I'm just so happy for you, Mofe. Congratulations." Then she buried her face in his chest and wept.

His heart fell. She didn't love him.

"Yeah, thanks," He muttered absent-mindedly, his heart torn in two.

"Let me see you off then," she said and quickly stepped to the front door. But he lingered in the room.

"Gracie, I wanted to…"

"Mofe, you should get going now. It's a great night to propose," she said with false cheer, opening the door wide for him, so he had no choice but to follow her out.

Seconds later, after he had driven off, she ran straight to her bed and sobbed her heart out.

Mofe drove home in a daze. As soon as he went through the front door, Margaret rushed at him.

"Oh my God, I've been so worried. You left your mother's house eight hours ago! Where have you been? What happened to your phone?"

He wanted to lie, but he decided not to. He decided that the lies stopped there and then. He couldn't keep lying to someone he was going to spend the rest of his life with. "I went to the beach, and from there I went to see Grace. Sorry, I left my phone in the car," he explained.

She looked at him for a moment and then sighed.

"You really got me scared. How is Grace?" She asked tiredly.

"She's doing fine. Margaret, I need to ask you a question."

"Okay?"

"Will you marry me?" He asked, taking her hand and bringing it to his lips.

"What? Do you mean that?" she asked in surprise, a smile curving her lips.

"I do. Let's get married and grow old together."

Margaret threw back her head and laughed happily.

"Of course, I will, Mofe. I will marry you," she answered feelingly and they hugged.

He brought out the ring he had bought, knelt in front of her and fitted it on her finger. Then he got up, pulled her to him and kissed her.

She was so excited that she began to immediately call everyone to tell them about the good news.

Mofe laughed. After listening to her place a few calls, he excused himself and went to his study where he locked himself in, put on some music and wept.

PLANS WERE MADE towards the wedding. Margaret was her own chief organizer. No one could organize her wedding better than she could, so she declined offers from friends and family to help. She left no stone unturned in her pursuit of the perfect wedding.

She asked Grace to be one of her bridesmaids. Grace agreed.

She warned Mofe to stay away, he knew nothing. He gladly left her alone. She chose everything: the cake, the dress, the suit, all of it. And Mofe didn't mind one bit.

A few weeks before the wedding, Mofe ran into Grace at an auction sale. Although they chose to sit together, they barely spoke throughout the event. At the end of the auction, they decided to get some lunch together. It was only then that they spoke. Grace was the one to break the ice after seeing how tired Mofe looked.

'"Mofe, are you okay? Do you even sleep at all?" She couldn't help asking.

"Yeah, I am. Just a little tired from all the wedding preparations. Otherwise, I'm great," he answered. "I should be asking you the same thing. You look a bit tired yourself."

*I would. I cry every night.*

"Yeah, work has been a bit hectic, but I am okay. Please, take me home. I really am so tired," she said and yawned.

"Aight. Let's go." He stood up and held out his hand to her. She put her hand in his and let him pull her up.

Then he took her home and stayed with her.

They talked for a while.

"Do you think there's just one right person for everyone?" Grace asked in a quiet voice.

"What do you mean?" He straightened up.

"I mean, when you have all these feelings for someone…

and you believe that he's the one for you. Everything about this person pleases you…when even their most annoying habits are endearing to you…I mean, if you feel that way about him, shouldn't he feel the same way about you? Shouldn't your heart and *his* beat together? Shouldn't he know somehow that you love him and desire to be with him forever? Shouldn't he ask that you be with him forever?" Grace's voice was shaky.

Mofe looked at her like he had seen a ghost. But she wasn't looking at him. Her eyes were gazing at something unseen, far away in the distance. When Mofe finally found his voice, it was husky and soft.

"Well, there are many kinds of people in the world. Some do find hearts that are in tune with theirs, some don't. I don't think it's possible that there's only one person for another, even though it may seem so sometimes. You know, you think that without that person in your life you would never be happy or feel complete, but I think that with time you get over those feelings, that emotional tie becomes frayed if not completely broken and you find strength to move on and find someone else whose heart beats with yours. There's always a way out. Sometimes we just have to believe that."

"I guess," Grace said in a small voice, wiping the tears away from her face.

"Please, don't cry, Grace. I can't bear to see you cry, you know that." His voice shook as he pulled her to him.

She stayed in his arms, crying softly, while he whispered comforting words to her.

After a while, she pulled away to look at him intensely.

"Do you think a person should continue being who they

have been all their life? Should they hold on to a certain trait they know they should discard for the sole reason that it makes them hurt other people and themselves as well?"

"No, I don't. I think changing for the better is a must," he answered.

"I don't want to be a coward anymore, Mofe. I can't continue like this." She stood up and paced up and down, arms flailing.

"What's the problem, Grace? Is it Maxwell?" He asked forcefully.

She stopped pacing and looked at him, "No, Mofe. It's not Maxwell. It is you. I am hopelessly in love with you. I've been in love with you for as long as I can remember but I couldn't say anything because I didn't know if you could love me back and I didn't want to spoil what we have and I've been in torment since you started dating Margaret and now you are marrying her and I'm going to end up all old, withered and alone," she sobbed uncontrollably.

Mofe was in too much shock to respond at first. Eventually, he found his wits and held her by the shoulders so she could hold still.

"Gracie, did you just say that you love me?" He had to be dreaming.

"Mofe. I love you with all that I am. I truly love you. I don't know if anything can happen anymore but I just needed to stop being such a coward and tell you how I feel."

"Gracie, I am the worst coward that ever lived because I've loved you since I was eight. I love you too, with everything in me. I tried many times to tell you, but, just like you, I was too afraid to ruin things. Oh my God, Gracie, you are my everything.

All that I need and want. I love you." He pulled her to him and planted his lips on hers.

And she responded with great fervour.

"Oh my goodness, Grace. I can't believe I'm kissing you," he said, whispering in her mouth.

"Oh, me neither, Mofe. Me neither," she whispered.

And they remained that way, kissing like two lovers who had been apart from each other for too long. In a way, that's exactly what it was.

Mofe kissed Grace the way he had never kissed anyone before. At first, it was with urgency, but then he realized that he was kissing the love of his life; the only woman he was in love with and he slowed it down and kissed her softly, delicately. He nibbled on her lips like they were tidbits, and then later deepened the kiss.

He cupped her face in the palm of his hands and looked deeply into her eyes. Grace caught her breath at the raw longing there, and suddenly, she found herself swept away from reality, carried on a tidal wave of emotion. When he started touching her, she was lost. He touched her like she was a delicate china. The full force of his feelings for her churning within him and for a moment he was breathless. He knew then that come what may, he would always love this girl, Grace, who had held on to his heart for as long as he could remember. This girl who had made his life worthwhile growing up. This girl who welcomed him as a lover, even though she had only known him as a friend.

He just knew he would harm anyone who messed with her, and that included himself.

So, he stopped kissing her and held her in a hug until she stopped quivering and quieted down.

When she finally looked at him with a questioning look in her eyes, he tried to explain.

"I'll live to regret this, but we have to stop, my love. A least for now," he smiled wryly at her, brushing her hair away from her face.

"No, no, no, we can continue," she said, massaging his strong arms.

"Believe me, darling, nothing would please me more, but I'm engaged to be married. I can't start up something new with someone else when there's someone in my life. Although, it doesn't feel at all new with you because we've known each other forever but... I need to take care of some things before we can, you know, love each other properly," he explained.

"I know. You are so amazing, Mofe." She looked up at him adoringly.

"You mean I'm such a loser?"

"Not at all, darling. You are a good man. You always try to do the right thing and I can't get over that."

"Yeah. That's the way it should be. We shouldn't hurt others when we know we can avoid it. And when we can't we should endeavour to make the pain as easy as possible and that means ripping off the Band-Aid swiftly. You shouldn't string someone along when you know they have no place in your life. Just tell them it's over so that they can move on."

"True, like I told Maxwell," she said distantly.

"Sweetie, I have to go now."

Grace nodded. "Are you going to tell her tonight?"

"Yes, I am. I'm going to tell her tonight." And he smiled.

"Okay, good. You'll let me know, right?" She sounded like a child.

"Yes, right away, babe," he assured her.

"Okay."

They walked to his car together where she watched hi drive off, waving him goodbye, a satisfied smiled plastered on her lips.

---

Mofe called his mother as soon as he drove out of Grace's compound.

"Mama, she loves me back. Grace loves me," He babbled excitedly.

"Oh, that is wonderful news, my son. Ah, my joy is full now. I am happy for you." He could hear the smile in her voice.

"Yes. So, I'm going to tell Margaret right away that we can't get married anymore."

"Hmmm. Do it gently. Make sure she knows that it is not her fault at all," his mother advised him.

"Yes, I know, Mama," he replied.

"But you have spent so much on the wedding preparations already. Will all that money go to waste?" His mother said, obviously concerned.

"Mama, it's all my money," he said. "I didn't allow her to spend a dime of hers. I don't care about the money."

"Okay. Hmmm. Anyway, you get back to me, alright?"

"I will, Mama."

As Mofe drove into his house, he just knew something was wrong because Margaret was standing by the front door, looking agitated.

He got out of the car and walked up to her. She was looking pale.

"What's wrong?" He asked her with a frown.

"Mofe, I am pregnant!"

"What?" He couldn't hide the shock on his face.

"Let's go inside, please," she said softly.

He looked at her for a moment, and then followed her inside.

"Pregnant? Margaret, how is that possible?" He asked as soon as the door shut behind them.

"I know, right? I'd been feeling under the weather for some time now, so I went to the clinic today. The doctor ran some tests and promised to call with the results. I just got off the phone with him a couple of minutes ago."

This was not possible.

"But we've been using condoms, Margaret."

"That's what I told the doctor! Apparently, no method of birth control is one hundred percent effective, but then we already know that so…"

"This is incredible!' Mofe exclaimed, his expression that of disbelief."

"Yes, I felt the same way until I remembered that we'd be getting married soon, which means I won't even show until months after our wedding," she smiled uneasily.

Mofe rubbed his hand over his head. "Margaret, that doesn't even hold water. If it did, we might as well have forgotten about using the damn condoms the minute that I proposed. We didn't say we would start having kids right away, did we? Hell, we've never even talked about having kids, have we?'

"You watch your words, Mister! I will not condone any swearing around here. So what are you saying? You are obviously not happy about this recent development. Should I go and get an abortion? Is that what you want?' She asked coldly.

"No!" he yelled at her and she jumped back in shock.

He took a deep breath, and in a calmer voice said,

"No, I didn't say that. You just hit me with something totally unexpected, Margaret. You don't expect me to jump for joy, do you? Let me adjust to this, please. Excuse me." And with that, he side-stepped her and went straight to his study where he locked himself in and slumped in one of the leather chairs in the room.

"Now, this is more like it," he hissed in frustration.

He just knew that the time spent with Grace had been too good to be true. Especially since he had always suspected that he was destined to suffer. He was destined to be in bondage, not head over heels in love. What had he been thinking? All he wanted was to be someone else. Maybe a nicer Maxwell. Anybody but himself.

He sat there in the dark for hours, thinking about what to do. In the end, he knew only one thing to do: the right thing.

He dragged himself up from the chair and went to look for Margaret. He found her lying in his bed reading a book.

'Hey," he said from the doorway.

"Hey," she sat up, closing the book.

He walked into the room and sat beside her. Then he took her hand in his.

"I'm sorry for the way I acted earlier. I was just... Anyway, I am sorry." "Apology accepted."

"Thank you," he said softly, bringing her hand to his lips.

He sat that way for a while, silently holding her hand in his. He seemed to be struggling with something.

"Are you okay?" She asked.

"Sure, I'm okay," but she could see the tears in his eyes.

"'You are crying, Mofe"

"Yes, I am. That's because I'm so glad I'm going to be a father." He smiled at her through his tears.

"Oh, me too. I can't wait."

"Yeah," he nodded, and the tears flowed freely.

"Oh baby, come here," she pulled him to her.

He rested his head in her bosom and cried from the terrible pain of what he had to let go of.

Across town, Grace lay awake in bed, waiting for the call that would open the door to her paradise. She imagined how it would be to be free to love Mofe. She imagined long walks on the beach, trips around the country, art galleries, auctions, movies, sex, sex, and more sex. Babies. A lovely boy who would look just like Mofe. Then the prettiest twin girls.

She felt the warmth in her thoughts permeate through every fibre of her being. Never had she felt this good. She had never truly experienced love like this. There was a time when she had started to think that she was born for pain. Mofe and his mother had been the only people who had genuinely cared about her. No one else. She barely remembered her parents. And if it were not for the fact that Mofe's mother had kept pictures of her parents and showed them to her often, she thought she would have forgotten about them entirely.

The only thing she remembered about her mom were the last few days they spent together before she died. No, before she killed herself.

"Back to pleasant thoughts!" she reprimanded herself.

She looked at the clock again and wondered why it was

taking so long for Mofe to call her. Breaking up with someone wasn't that hard a thing to do, so she didn't understand why it was taking such a long time.

Well, she would just lie down patiently and wait for his call. She was excited at the prospect of hearing his darling voice again.

She fell asleep with a sweet smile on her face.

In the morning, when she awoke, there was a text message waiting for her.

"I'm so sorry, Grace," was all it said.

---

THE NEXT FEW days rushed by in a blur. Grace had never been so stupefied in her whole life. She called Mofe to get an explanation from him but all he had said was that he would come and see her.

When he finally announced that he was coming over to see her, she waited for him with her heart in her mouth.

She rushed into his arms the moment he came in and he held her tightly to himself as if he would die if he let her go.

He found her lips and kissed her desperately.

Okay. He was kissing her. Everything was fine.

She clung to him, her knees weak.

"Oh, I missed you, Grace. I missed you so badly," he whispered into her mouth.

"Oh, my darling, you have no idea," she whispered back and dug her tongue deep into his mouth.

She pressed herself against him, willing their bodies to be joined as one, and he groaned deeply, holding her even tighter.

"Mofe, what happened?" She asked in a whisper.

Her question brought him back to his senses. He stopped kissing her and led her to the sofa. They sat down, facing each other.

"Gracie, we need to talk."

"I was so scared when I read your message and then you came in and started kissing me and I was like, 'yay', but now, I'm scared again," she said, nervousness written on her face.

"She's pregnant, Grace. Margaret is carrying my baby."

"What?"

"I know," he said tiredly.

"What does this mean? How does this affect us?" she asked.

Mofe was silent for a while and then he exhaled and said, "I have to marry her, Grace. I can't have a child outside of wedlock. I just can't." And he shook his head.

"What? Marry her? What about me? I love you!"

"And I love you, but I've come to realize that sometimes love is not enough," he said in a low voice.

"That's all I get? Philosophy?" She asked bitterly.

"Gracie, please try to understand," he pleaded.

"Understand what? That you awakened my feelings and now you wanna run? How do you want me to understand that?" She yelled at him.

"Believe me, Gracie, I wanna stick to you like glue. If I had my way, there's no way I would ever leave you, ever! But this is bigger than me. It's bigger than you. It's bigger than us. This is a child we are talking about. An innocent child who was conceived through no fault of his. He's going to need a father to welcome him into the world as he's pushed out of the womb. He's going to need a father to teach him a whole lot of stuff; how to do a lot of stuff. Children are better off with both parents than with just one," he said.

"Seriously? You don't need to get married to her to be able to do all that with your child, Mofe. I had two parents, Mofe. *You remember*, you were there. I had two parents and if it wasn't for *your single mother*, I would probably be on my knees right now, seeing to the debased needs of all kinds of men at very odd hours of the night, but I am not there because your mother took better care of me than my own bloody parents did. I was better off without my parents. *You do remember,* right?" She snarled.

"I do, Grace, but it doesn't feel right for me to abandon Margaret right now. She needs me and I want to be there for her and our kid. I'm really sorry."

"So, your mind is made up, then?" She asked him with tears gathering in her eyes.

"It is, I'm so sorry, Gracie." He looked at her with deeply sad eyes.

She got up and knelt before him, her tears falling fast.

"What if I said *please*? Huh? What if I told you that living without you would mean the end of me? What if I told you that life began to smile at me from the moment you kissed me? What if I told you that I look forward to spending my life with you, to sharing the tiniest details with you? What if I told you that if you left me, I won't ever stop crying because I won't ever get over you? What if I told you that to me you are life, you are the air that I breathe? What if I told you that you are me and I am you? What if I told you that I would gladly give up my brushes, canvas, colors, all for you? That I would never paint again if you would stay with me? That I would gladly live my life for you? That living without you would mean damnation for me? What if I told you all of these things and I meant them from the depth of my heart? Would it change anything? Would your heart be moved at all? Please?" her nails dug into his jean-clad thighs.

Mofe couldn't help the tears that gushed out of his eyes at her words. He was dumbfounded as he realized again how brave this woman was. He felt unworthy, and rightfully so. Grace was the most wonderful woman he had ever known.

He had always known she was an amazing person, but this was extraordinarily amazing. He had never known her like this before.

Rising to his feet, he pulled her up from her kneeling position, drew her to him and wrapped his arms around her. He just held her that way, rocking from side to side.

Different sweet smells assailed his nostrils; from her hair to her skin. She smelled exactly the way she was; incredibly sweet, and it made him want to do beautiful things to her.

"Gracie, I understand. I understand because I feel the same way, exactly the same way. I don't even know how I'm going to live the rest of my life with someone else, knowing I could have spent it with wonderful you. And I know I would surely stop breathing if you got married to someone else knowing it could have been me. It hurts me already, but I don't see any way around it, so I'm begging you to please understand," he whispered as he continued to rock her.

"There's no way I can understand that right now. I can't!" She cried

"I have to be there for Margaret. This is my child we're talking about here, Baby. I want to be as involved in his life as possible.

I want him to see me before he sleeps and wake up to me as well. I don't know, but knowing that a part of me is growing inside of her has humbled me. I've never treated her badly, but right now, I really want to do right by her and our child. Please, baby."

"So, you really have made up your mind, huh?" she asked, her face expressionless.

"I'm afraid so," he nodded soberly.

"Okay then," she nodded as well, stepping away from him. She wrapped her arms around herself as she felt a chill in her heart.

"Please, leave now," she said quietly.

"Gracie, please," he said.

"Don't, please. Just go. I need to lie down," she said, her face clouded.

"Okay, I will go, but promise me that you will call me if you need anything."

She just stared at him with vacant eyes. He looked at her for a while and then turned and left.

Grace locked the door after him and went into her bedroom where she found a thick sweater and put it on. Then she climbed into bed and wrapped her duvet around herself.

Her mother was right. It is only in death that anyone can find peace and happiness.

---

MOFE TOLD HIS mother about the latest development and the stand he had taken.

"My son, I will go with whatever you choose. I really hoped

that you and Grace would get married, however, I am very proud of your decision and I will try to help Grace understand," she said.

"Mama, please take care of her for me, please." He still hurt from what he had had to do to her.

"I will do my best, Mofe," His mother promised him.

---

AS THEIR WEDDING day drew near, Mofe became even more convinced that he had made the right decision. Margaret had become softer and more emotional. She would burst into tears for no reason. She would vomit until there was nothing left in her stomach. There was no way he could have been able to justify leaving her in her condition.

He made it a point to spend as much time with her as he could. He hated to leave her alone in his apartment. He held her when she vomited and mopped her sweaty brow afterwards. He took care of her as best as he could.

Grace stopped taking his calls. At first, he kept calling, but one day she answered and asked him if he had changed his mind.

"No, Grace, I haven't," he had answered quietly.

"Then why are you calling me?"

"I just want to know how you're doing. I'm very worried about you."

"I'm not your responsibility anymore, Mofe. Margaret is. You chose her over me, so focus on her and leave me the hell alone!" She had yelled angrily and hung up.

So he left her alone but not after urging his mother to always check on Grace.

Grace felt more alone than she had ever been in her whole life. It felt like she was the unhappiest person in the world. She couldn't eat, couldn't paint. She just wanted to lie in bed.

To make matters worse, she began to hear her late mother's voice more and more. Especially the things she had said to her before she died. And the death scene kept replaying in her mind.

Her mother had spread some pills on her dresser and invited her to help her count them.

"Bisi, come over here and let's see how well you can count now," her mother had said with a plastic smile on her face.

Grace had obeyed.

"I think the pills here are about a hundred but I am not sure, so I want you to help me count, okay?"

Grace had nodded.

"Okay! We'll play a game now. If you count ten pills correctly, I will reward you by swallowing all ten, okay?"

"Yes, Mother."

"Good girl! Now count."

She had counted ten pills and her mother had swallowed them and cheered with glee. She did it like that until she counted all hundred pills correctly. Her mother swallowed them all.

After their game, her mother had curled up on her bed and began to talk to her about how death was the only ticket to peace and happiness. She told her that life was too hard, so in order to be free, death was the only option.

"Grace, promise me that when life gets too hard, that you will do as I have done, you will seek peace and happiness. Promise me." her mother had slurred.

"I promise, Mother," she had said with tears in her eyes.

And then she had watched as her mother breathed her last. She had been in a state of shock and had been unable to call out for help.

She had been unable to move and had blacked out eventually until she was rescued.

All her life, she had shoved that incident down into the deepest part of her mind and she had never revisited it. Not once after it happened. So, it was eerie that everything was so clear to her now.

At the end of it all, her mother was right. She had nothing to live for. Mofe had decided to abandon her for someone else. She had to find her own happiness and she knew only one way to do that.

Over the next few days, she thought of going her mother's way. She would walk into a drugstore to try and find the same pills her mother had used to find happiness. But instead, she would trudge aimlessly up and down every aisle and eventually she would leave without any purchase.

She wanted to end her life, but she didn't know how to. She felt like such a coward each time she left a drugstore without a purchase.

"A coward I am, a coward I will always be. Just like I was with Mofe. If I had professed my love to him a year ago, we would have been together by now. I would have been the pregnant girl he wants to stand by. But no, I chose to keep mute and now my destiny is tampered with. I'm a big coward, the biggest coward that ever lived." She would chide herself over and over again.

Until one day, she decided that come what may, she would get the pills. She was about to enter the pharmacy when someone called her name. She turned around and saw Ekene. Ekene was Mofe's good friend and best man.

"This is just great," she muttered under her breath, before walking to him.

"Hi, Grace." He smiled, stretching out his hand for a handshake.

"Ekene. Hi."

They shook hands and exchanged more pleasantries.

"So, what did you come to get?" he asked her.

The question threw her off guard. She hadn't prepared to meet anyone she knew there, let alone answer any question so her mind was blank. She finally blurted out the first thing that came to her mind.

"Condoms."

"Condoms?" he raised a brow.

*Condoms? Oh great, Grace.*

"Yes, condoms," she repeated.

"Oh, that's cool! I came to get some vitamins," he offered.

*Vitamins! That's what you should have said, Grace.*

"Oh, nice," she said absent-mindedly.

He held the door for her and she stepped in. He followed and motioned her over to the aisle he thought she was looking for.

"You seem to know your way around here," she said knowingly.

"I do," he laughed. "I live just around the corner. I'm also an adult."

"Of course. Well, thanks for showing me the way. You take care now."

"It's fine. I'll just wait for you," he offered.

*Oh my goodness!*

"Suit yourself," she muttered with apparent irritation as she snatched a pack from the shelf.

"Are you sure that one pack is enough?" he asked with a blank look on his face.

"You are probably right," she answered through clenched teeth and grabbed two more packs before hurrying away from the aisle. She felt him following briskly.

She got to the counter and brought out her purse.

"Hey, put that away! I'm paying," he announced.

"No, I can't let you do that. I should pay."

"Oh, loosen up, Grace. Have fun on me." He had a devilish glint in his eyes now, and if she hadn't been so mortified, she would have laughed out loud.

She conceded and he paid the bill.

"Your vitamins; aren't you going to get them?" she asked.

"Ah, don't worry. I still have plenty left at home. Let me see you off."

He escorted her to her car and waved as she drove off.

She decided to find another means of finding happiness because her mother's way was clearly not the path.

After hours of wracking her brain, she finally decided to let go of the plan to end her life. Maybe she wasn't meant to walk the same path as her mother. The pain was terrible, though. She missed Mofe every day and prayed he would change his mind and return to her. She had no idea how she was going to attend the wedding. She was even in the wedding! She had to get out of that particular errand because there was no way she was going to stand by and watch Mofe get married to another woman. It would kill her in a way she had never died before.

She had to speak with Margaret and despite the fact that her heart hurt as she did it, she gave Margaret a call.

"Grace, where have you been?" was Margaret's question as soon as she answered.

"I've been really busy. I'm even calling with bad news."

"What happened?"

"I can't be at the wedding, I'm sorry," Grace said.

"Why not? What happened?" she droned and Grace winced.

"I have to go out of town for business. It's really important so I can't get out of it, I'm sorry."

"Seriously? Oh, Mofe would be so crushed."

"Yeah. I'm really sorry, Margaret. I'll call you soon, please. I have to go now," she said and hung up.

"Oh, thank God!" she breathed with relief.

That was done. Next item on the list. Relocation.

When Mofe heard that Grace wasn't going to attend his wedding, he broke down. That was when he realized how much he had hurt her. Grace was usually so mellow and lenient. She never could hold on to negative energy so he knew for sure that she was badly hurt, and he feared what she might do next. He knew she would do something drastic and he needed to stop her.

He drove to her place early the next morning and banged on her door.

She flung it open a couple of minutes later and when she saw that it was him, she tried to shut the door but he was quicker than she was. He put his foot through the door and even though it hurt, he was able to stop her from jamming it. He forced himself into the house and shut the door behind them.

"What do you want here, Mofe? Why don't you leave me alone?" she yelled at him.

"I am sorry, Grace, I can't leave you alone. I am deeply sorry for causing you pain, but it shouldn't be the end of the world for you. You need to believe that there's someone out there who would love you better than me. You need to get on with your life, despite the hurt, just as I'm trying to do!"

"Yeah, right!" she snorted.

"Oh, you think I'm not heartbroken?"

"You are not, Mofe. If you were, you would be with me in a heartbeat!" she replied stubbornly.

"Oh, believe me, I am heartbroken. You have no idea how heartbroken I am. The moments I spend in my study are spent with you. I trace my fingers over your painting on my wall. I talk to you through that painting. Tell me you don't hear my voice sometimes. Tell me you don't hear me cry sometimes. Tell me you don't feel my touch every day. That is where I connect with you every day. That is where I can be alone with you. I miss you, with every fibre of my being. It's still so unbelievable that I can't be with you." His voice broke.

Grace let the tears run down her face as he spoke. He spoke the truth for she did feel him with her every day, all the time. She realized how difficult it was for him to be with someone and yearn for another. She understood that, but she just found it hard to accept that there was nothing he could do; that there was nothing either one of them could do about it.

"Mofe, are you sure there's nothing we can do? What if you talked to Margaret? I'm sure she would understand and let you go."

"I can't do that, Grace. I don't want to do that. I want to be there for her and our baby. It doesn't matter that I am not deeply in love with her. I made love to her and got her pregnant, so I must stand up to my responsibility. I must do right by her and my child," he insisted as she cried silently.

"Gracie, please, I need you to get on with your life. I love you too much to watch you suffer. You deserve to be happy, and if you allow yourself, you'll find happiness with someone else, a much better person than me."

"No, Mofe, that's the problem. There's no one else like you. Not to me, there isn't. I can't think of anyone who would be to me what you are. The bar is too high," she wailed.

"Okay, why don't you use me to measure all future boyfriends? There may not be someone exactly like me, but you could find someone close or even much better."

"No! I can't. I can't watch you love another woman, live with her, be her husband, do everything with her. I cannot!" she cried bitterly.

Mofe was silent while she cried. He didn't dare to go near her for he would not be able to control himself. He would not be able to hold back from kissing her, so he stood afar while she wept. She calmed down eventually and looked up at him with her wet, brown eyes.

"Really, Mofe, I can't watch you live your life with someone else. I would just die!"

"Then you would understand how many times I died each time you were in a relationship with those other guys," he said quietly.

"What?" She was stunned.

"I went through all your past relationships with you. And even though it hurt me deeply, I stood by you whenever you fell apart. I comforted you whenever they hurt you. I watched you live your life with them even though it killed me to do so. You said you won't be able to do it, so I want you to remember in your quiet moments that I did it for you. Over and over again."

And with that, he walked up to her, hugged her tightly, pressed his lips to her forehead and left.

---

THREE DAYS TO the wedding, someone rang the doorbell to Mofe's house. Margaret was the one who answered it. There stood Grace, smiling hesitantly.

"Hey, what a lovely surprise!" Margaret hugged her affectionately. "Mofe, Grace is here," she called out as she ushered her in.

"What's going on here?" Mofe walked towards them and then stopped in his tracks when he saw Grace.

"Grace!" he exclaimed

"Hi, Mofe. I just came to ask if I can still be in the wedding. I was able to get out of the trip," she said quickly.

"Yay!" Margaret yelled gleefully and then suddenly burst into tears and ran into the bedroom.

"What happened? Why is she crying?" Grace asked in a panic.

"Mood swings. It's pregnancy hormones. I'll be right back," Mofe whispered to her.

"Oh, okay," Grace said with relief.

A while later, they both came out and Margaret smiled at Grace sheepishly.

"I'm sorry about that, Grace. I can count how many times I've cried my whole life, so I guess God is paying me back for that now." They all laughed.

Margaret gave Grace an up-to-date report on the upcoming wedding and Mofe made them dinner. After dinner, Grace and Mofe did the dishes while Margaret regaled them with more gist about the wedding.

Until eventually she pleaded tiredness and went in to lie down.

"What's happening, Grace?" Mofe asked Grace after Margaret had left.

"First of all, I'm so sorry for all that I put you through in the past. I realize now how much of a pain I was then. I'm so sorry. Secondly, I want to say congratulations on your wedding and unborn baby. I mean it from the bottom of my heart. Thirdly, I'm not over you yet, but I have decided to let you go because it's for the greater good. And I promise you that I will look at the possibilities in life now. I will open up and find a way to be happy. I will take responsibility for my life now, take care of myself more, and just be happy. That's what I'm going to do." She spoke softly.

"Wow! That's the most impressive speech I've heard in a long time, Gracie. Although, I'm a little sad that you are letting me go but I'm glad you have decided to try to be happy. I'm so grateful for that Gracie because you just gave me renewed strength to carry on. The prospect of being a father scares me silly, Grace," he confessed.

"No. I think you're going to be the most wonderful father ever."

"Really?"

"Oh yes, really! I have no doubt about that at all."

"Okay. That makes me feel so much better. Thank you, Grace," he said.

"No, thank you, Mofe," she countered and they smiled at each other.

---

THE WEDDING WAS beautiful. Everything went smoothly. After the vows were said, there was not a dry eye in the church. Grace couldn't stop the flow of tears from her eyes as she watched her Mofe get married. She was happy and sad at the same time. Ekene offered her his handkerchief and she was surprised at how clean it was.

The reception was superb. Everything was beautifully organized, thanks to Margaret. Not a single thing was out of place. Indeed, it was the perfect wedding.

Grace was sitting in her seat nursing her drink when Ekene walked up to her.

"Beautiful wedding, eh?" he said.

"It really is. When I'm getting married, I'm calling Margaret," she said with a laugh.

"That makes two of us," he smiled.

He hovered for a minute and then said, "Care to dance?"

She was starting to decline when she remembered that she was supposed to be making herself happy, so she accepted. Ekene led her to the floor and put one arm around her waist, while he took her hand in his. They moved to the slow number.

"Grace?" he said hesitantly.

"Yes, Ekene?"

"You smell nice."

"Thank you, Ekene."

"You are welcome."

And they kept on dancing.

"Grace?"

"Hmmm?" she was starting to relax in his arms.

"I've always wanted to ask you out on a date."

"Really? Why didn't you?"

"Because of your closeness to Mofe. Thank God he is out of the way now."

"Okay."

"So, when?"

"When what?"

"When are we having the date? Next week? Tomorrow? Now?"

"Now?' she looked at him in surprise. 'The wedding isn't over."

"Oh, for goodness sake, it is. Margaret and Mofe have started their happily ever after. I think we should work towards starting ours," he complained.

"What?"

"Just pick a day, Grace. Now is a great idea." He looked hopeful.

She laughed heartily. "Now is not a good time, no." She shook her head.

"Oh okay." He sounded disappointed.

She moved closer and rested her head on his shoulder.

"How about tomorrow?"

"Yes! What time? 6:00 a.m.?"

This time, she couldn't hold back the ripple of laughter that coursed through her body. It was a beautiful sound to his ears.

"Where could we possibly go on a date at six in the morning?"

"I'll show you, Grace. It's a beautiful place," he said, looking deep into her eyes.

"Okay then, 6:00 a.m. it is," she answered, mesmerized.

"Grace?"

"Hmmm?"

"Did you really go to that drugstore to get condoms?"

"No, I didn't."

"Great, Grace. Just great," he said softly.

Yes, great. He had saved her from killing herself that day. He was her saviour. She rested her head back on his shoulder and smiled happily.

# 4
# BRODA AZAYA

### *Dedication*

FOR EMMANUEL EBESUNUN,
ONAKOYA SEYI , CELESTINA OMENEKI-GOLD,
PATRICK ANYAFULU, SAMMY OMOTESE,
ADAKU SOPH, CUE MELODY, CHIEF SLY,
TEMIDAYO AHANMISI, LADY TINA UWADIAE,
KINGSLEY UKAOHA, BLESSING EBIEME,
MEDEME OVWE, CHARLES MADUEKE AND TO
ALL NAIJA LAFFERS.

I LOVE YOU GUYS. THANK YOU FOR
EVERYTHING.

I was 13 years when everything started happening all at once. First, my father fell sick and stopped going out to drink as was his normal practice. He had a bad cough and when he coughed he sounded like an old motorcycle struggling to come alive. He would wheeze for a long time and then stop as if catching his breath before he continued again. After coughing for a few minutes, he would spit out thick, discoloured phlegm. Then his breathing would become laboured and I would have to get him some water to calm him down. Most days, I would sit on the floor in a corner of our room and just watch him as he lay on the bed fighting for breath. I didn't need anyone to tell me he was very sick. My maternal grandmother used to say that his drinking would one day lead him to his death and I often wondered how that would happen.

---

ON THE DAY the village herbalist came to treat my father, I was driven out of the room by my mother who had managed to take time out of her trading to be there. I heard her urging the herbalist to hurry up so that she could go back to her stall at the market. My mother sold vegetables at the village market and my father drank every day. The hard life took away my mother's mirth, if there was even any in her before. She would curse my father at the slightest provocation. My mother fed the house, paid my school fees and bought me used clothes. All my father ever did was drink with his friends from dawn until dusk, then he would stagger home, ignore my mother's nagging while he talk with me for a few minutes and then fall into bed and snore till noon the next day. But I loved him, because he showed interest in me.

I stood there, afraid and shaken to my roots. I knew something was wrong; something that was beyond even my mother's control. That was alarming because she was always in control of everything. I felt goose bumps all over my body as I heard the herbalist's chants and incantations. I felt so scared and lonely because I had no one to talk to. I had no siblings and I had no real friends as well. Growing up, I was a frail child, very small for my age and I never spoke in class, so no one wanted to play with me. I stood by the corner and listened to every sound that came from the room. I let every word sink into me until I began to hear the sounds from within me. I became nauseated and dizzy and I held on to the wall for support. My only companion was my father, who was fighting for his life. I wished someone would hold me and comfort me. I began to think about how good my father had been to me. He spent only a couple of minutes with me each day, but those few minutes meant the world to me because that was the only time someone bothered about me.

I began to pray that my father would get well because I didn't want to be alone. Even on his sickbed, he still managed to look after me and I cherished that so much. Those few moments I got to spend with him every day meant the whole world to me. I was startled out of my thoughts by a shrill scream from my father, and I started shaking again. I was torn between going in there to check what was going on and staying back to avoid whatever was going on. I felt nauseated and I vomited all over the floor. My mother must have suspected something was wrong outside because in a moment, she was by my side.

"Wetin be this, Ufuoma?" She asked, placing her hand against my forehead to feel my temperature. "Your body no dey hot na. Why you vomit for ground? Oya, carry broom make you sweep am now now, otherwise I go beat shit comot from your body. Make you and your yeye papa no go kill me for this house," she complained angrily.

"Mama, I hear," I ran inside to get a broom. By this time, the herbalist had finished with his incantations and was sitting quietly in the only chair in our room. I avoided looking straight at my father but I could see from the corner of my eye that he was lying motionless on the bed. I collected the broom and ran outside to do what my mother had asked me to. It only took a few minutes and I rinsed out the broom and took it back to the room where I met the most amazing sight I'd ever seen in my life. My father was sitting up in bed and talking animatedly with the herbalist. I was so surprised that I ran to him and embraced him.

"Papa, you don well!" I said happily.

"Yes, my pikin, I don well," he laughed. "Oya, tell Chief thank you." I knelt before the herbalist and said an effusive thank you. Then I got up and went back outside. My mother was nowhere in sight. She had returned to her stall to continue with her sales.

I was happy for the rest of the day. I even escorted the herbalist a little and he told me to make sure my father didn't take the Ogogoro drink he usually took. I promised I would make sure he didn't take it ever again. I slept like a baby that night. I didn't have one single nightmare. When I woke up the next morning, my father was dead.

I was already up on my feet before my brain could register the cause of the loud wailing that woke me. I ran toward the sound and behold, it was my mother, sitting on the floor between Mama Kevwe, our neighbour, and my grandmother. She was weeping bitterly and the two women with her were trying to comfort her. At first I thought I was dreaming, because I had never seen my mother shed a tear before let alone wailing and hitting her hands on the floor. I stood rooted to one spot, confused by my mother's howling. And then I heard it...

"Shuo! Mamuro, na wetin na? That one na husband before? Wetin he dey do for your life before? Money for food, no! Cloth o, no! To pay school fees, for where! Na only drink he sabi drink. See, as he die so naim better pass."

I knew it was my grandmother talking. I could make out her deep, dry and gravelly voice.

My mother shouted, trying to jerk free from the two women holding her. "Mama, na still my husband o. My husband don die o. Make una see me o, my husband don die o!"

The world began to spin around me. My ears were ringing loudly and there was darkness everywhere. I tried to steady myself by stretching forth my hand to hold on to something, anything. But I felt nothing. I couldn't stand anymore so I let myself sink to the ground.

I began to hear the sound again. The chant and incantations of the old herbalist. The sound came from within me; went through my chest, up my throat and out of my mouth. It exploded in my ears. I heard his voice everywhere. It was painful. My ears hurt so bad that I began to claw at them. I heard a piercing shriek from somewhere within me, and then I felt wetness on my face and tightness in my chest, and some squeezing in there too.

My father was dead. He was dead. He had died while I was sleeping. From what, I didn't know because he was perfectly fine before I went to bed. I began to sob so loudly that my grandmother came to me and held me close. She looked sober. My mother wept louder when she saw me. Even Mama Kevwe joined in. I must have roused something in them to make them show such emotion because they hadn't acted this way when I first saw them with my mother.

"See pikin o, Oghene biko! How we go do this one na?" my grandmother lamented.

All of a sudden, I saw the old herbalist sitting in a corner and shaking his head. I felt anger, deep and hot as I rushed at him, hitting him over and over again with my tiny fists.

"Shuo, na wetin dey worry this wan? Wetin I do you?" he frowned in confusion.

"You say my papa don well but he still die. Na you kill my papa," I shouted at him, my fists clenched by my sides.

"Na me kill your papa? Or na you?" he snorted in disgust.

My whole body went still.

"Me? As I take kill my own papa?" my voice shook a little.

"I tell you make you no let am drink Ogogoro again, but you sleep forget the message I send you. Your papa drink Ogogoro last night and the medicine wey make am well no want Ogogoro at all. That's why he die. Who kill am so?" He sneered at me.

I remembered the instruction he had given me the previous evening. He had taken me aside to warn me seriously and I hadn't even remembered to carry it out. I never should have slept last night. I should have stayed up all night to make sure he never drank the dreaded Ogogoro. It was true. I killed my father. I killed him. I was responsible for his death.

"Na me kill am," I whispered, with hot tears running down my face.

"Eh hen, na so." He said nodding his head.

I turned and walked back inside the house, leaving my

mother, my grandmother and Mama Kevwe looking at me with pity in their eyes. None of them said anything to the herbalist, so I knew he was right that I had killed my father. I went into the room and found my corner. I sat there with my legs drawn up to my chin and my arms folded around them. I began to rock to and fro, thinking about how I was a murderer at thirteen.

*I killed my father!*

I began to sob quietly to myself. I felt pain so indescribable, so sharp and deep. I couldn't even think well. I just rocked and cried softly.

After the death of my father, life continued. Everyone and everything went back to normal. My mother stayed indoors for three months (it was surprising that she managed to do that considering how restless she was), according to tradition, and then she resumed her trading. My grandmother who had stayed with us for a couple of weeks went back to her own house.

For a whole month, my father's things were untouched. None of his relatives came asking for them; probably because they knew he had nothing of value. I always had an eerie feeling whenever I saw anything that belonged to him and I would almost jump out of my skin if I accidently touched any of it. For a long time, I wondered what to do about that, until one day, I decided on what to do. I gathered everything that belonged to him and stuffed them all into a garri sack. I tied the neck of the sack with a piece of string and kept it in a corner of the room, to take it to the poorest man in the village. I sat for some time, staring at the sack and wondering how I was going to be able to part with the only reminder of my dear late father. And then I heard his voice from within me...

"When you wan dash person something, no let the thing make yaga yaga give am. If na cloth you wan give person, you go press am, arrange am well. If na shoe, clean am make dirty no dey am. The person go happy like that. But if you give person scatter-scatter thing, the person go feel like small ant."

I nodded to myself, remembering when we had this particular conversation, and with tears streaming down my face I dragged the sack back to the middle of the room and brought everything out again.

I couldn't press the clothes but I made sure to fold them neatly. I got a clean rag and wiped clean my father's only shoe. I was straightening out the last pair of trousers when something fell out of its pocket. I looked down and saw that it was a bead that my father always wore around his wrist. I stared at it for a moment, surprised to find it amongst his things because he never, ever took it off. I never saw his dead body so before now I believed he'd been buried with it. Now, I knew someone had taken it off his wrist. Or had he removed it by himself? Could he have left it there for me to find? Had my father left me a keepsake? I could only wonder this within me.

I pondered on this for a while and then I decided to slip it on. It hung loosely around my wrist but I did not mind. I would ask my mother to help shorten the string later. I went back to the task before me, neatly folding each clothing item and transferring them into the sack. The shoe was the last thing to go in and I carefully put it on top of the clothes and then tied the neck of the sack again, this time painstakingly.

I took the sack containing all of my late father's possessions and took them to poor Papa Okiemute. He was one of my father's drinking mates whom my mother despised, so he was surprised to see me. He looked at me strangely when I told him my mission, but he accepted my charity and prayed for me.

I left there feeling very satisfied. I smiled to myself, flinging my slender arms as I walked away from Papa Okiemute's house. I suddenly realized that I felt happy for the first time in months. It was really good to be good as my father always said.

I decided to savour what I was feeling for a while, and that meant not going back home immediately. I walked round the village; stopping occasionally to stare long and hard at whatever caught my fancy.

I forgot to mention that the only striking thing about me were my eyes. They were bright and shiny, and if I hadn't been so timid I would have been able to stare anyone down.

I continued with my leisure walk around the village until it started to get dark. I started running home as I didn't want my mother to get home before me. When I got home, I noticed a rickety Raleigh bicycle parked in front. It was resting against the only tree in our compound. As I neared the front door, I heard a girly laugh, followed by happy shriek. It sounded like my mother but I couldn't believe it because she never laughed like this. Her laughter was either sarcastic or bitter, but like this? Never! I decided to find out what was happening so I walked into the room and what I saw gave me goose bumps.

A man was sitting on my father's bed with my mother on his lap. And she was indeed the person letting out all the giggles. I was angry. My vision became clouded and my face grew so hot that I thought it was going to explode. I let out a shrill scream and then I blacked out.

I came to slowly, and tried to open my eyes. There were voices calling my name I recognized my mother's voice and then, that of a strange man. My vision was hazy; I couldn't really make out my surroundings but I could make out his form and I felt angry again. I didn't want them to know I was conscious so I quickly shut my eyes tightly, listening to them argue about me.

"Mamuro, na which kind thing be this na? This your pikin na winsh o, shuo!" He exclaimed, pronouncing his 'ch' as 'sh'.

"She no be winsh. She neva see me wit anoda man before." my mother replied him.

"Abeg, I no fit do this kind thing, Mamuro," he said while pacing the small untidy room. "This your pikin no pure at all o."

"Shuo, you no know say I get pikin before? Wetin that one won mean na?"

"I no know say na dis kind pikin you get na! I no fit, abeg."

"No be you say you love me?" I could hear the hurt in my mother's voice.

"No vex, abeg. Love no dey dis one. I dey go. Abeg, no fine me o," his words were harsh and his steps sounded as if a million demons were after him.

"Shuo! Which kind man be this? Make he dey go sef!" She said to no one in particular.

By this time, I was fully conscious and I felt better; especially as I knew he was off my mother for good.

"Foma!" My mother said aloud as she bent over me.

"Ma," I replied weakly as I tried to get up.

My mother picked me off the floor and lay me on her bed. She went out and came back with a bowl of water and a clean rag which she dipped inside the water, squeezed dry and began to mop my face with.

"Foma, wetin make you collapse just na?" She asked me in a surprisingly gentle tone and for an instant I felt like I was in another world with a different mother. This wasn't my mother. My mother was harsh and impatient. This was pleasantly different and I felt good all over.

"Mama, I no like that man," I said tentatively and then held my breath, waiting for the outburst.

It never came. Instead she smiled and said, "No mind am. He no be beta person."

I looked at her face, she was tired but I could swear she looked beautiful with the smile. I couldn't remember seeing my mother smile the way she did at that moment and not at me. It drew me to her. I felt close to her, more than I ever did since I became conscious of myself as a human being. I decided that I liked the feeling and I was going to do everything in my power to preserve it.

My mother consulted the village herbalist about my fainting spell and he instructed her to take good care of me and to be mindful of the kind of men she brought home because as a child who had been close to her late father, it posed an adverse effect on me. He also said if I fainted whenever any man came around my mother, that would only mean that the man's intentions weren't honourable, so for the next few days, my mother showed me a lot of care.

She cooked my favourite meals and even bought me sweets; something she was usually very strict about. I revelled in her attention and care and I began to recover from my father's death. I didn't want to go back to having a very harsh and emotionally unavailable mother so my fainting spells became quite frequent.

Well, they happened whenever I saw my mother with a man. I made sure to faint in their presence, and that always succeeded in scaring them away. This went on for a long time, and within this time I grew taller and actually blossomed. My mother remained husbandless and I possessed a loving and caring mother. Men stayed away from my mother. None dared to come close to her anymore and it was all because of me. They even called me a witch, but I didn't care. As long as I was happy, I didn't care.

Until one day my mother brought a new man home. His name was Azaya , and he looked different from the other scruffy loafers who had been coming around my mother. My mother returned from the market one evening with him in tow, carrying her heavy load for her. He looked at me and smiled. He was the first of the men to actually see me and not look through me as was common with my mother's men. Unlike the others who paid no single attention to me.

"Madam, na your daughter be this?" he asked my mother, still smiling warmly at me.

"Yes, na my pikin. Ufuoma, make you salute brother na," my mother said uneasily, watching out for any sign of a swooning episode from me.

I looked at him, trying to gauge his intentions but couldn›t. I wasn›t sure if I should faint or not. I stood there watching while he walked up to me and then squatted before me, still smiling. I tried to stare him down but he smiled the more.

"Shuo, Madam, this your daughter fine o. See as her eyes dey shine like ajebutter pikin own. Fine girl, how are you?"

I mumbled something at him and raced inside, completely confused. No one had ever referred to me as 'fine' before. I was disconcerted, confused. I truly was thrown completely off-guard. I went to the window to spy at them and I saw nothing out of order. I stared at him; taking in his good looks, old but clean and neat clothes, and nice leather sandals. He was a good-looking man. He wasn't fat but he had some flesh on him. His skin wasn't dry like most of the men I knew. It was fresh and shiny. It was obvious he was very healthy. He looked nothing like my late father, who had always been thin and frail. I felt drawn to him all of a sudden. There was just something about him that made me want to know more about him. He was a big mystery to me.

I watched him talk to my mother a little bit more and then he bade her farewell but not without yelling, "Ufuoma, goodnight."

I didn't respond, I kept on spying through our threadbare curtain.

After that day, it became a tradition for Azaya to escort my mother home every evening, make small talk with her outside and head home. I saw no trace of romance between them, but I noticed that my mother looked happier. I had no just reason to faint because he didn't seem like a threat to me and to the memory of my late father. But I continued to watch him each day so as not to miss out on any form of romance between them. One day, my mother came back from the market early because she hadn't been feeling well. This I found out later, but I got home from school to find my mother in bed and Isaiah sitting next to her, talking in low, soft tunes. I wasted no time in letting out my famous shriek and slumping to the floor.

Nothing prepared me for what I saw when I regained consciousness. At first, I thought I was dreaming, because what I was saw was totally different from what I normally regained consciousness to. Normally, I would hear a low-toned but heated argument between my mother and her suitor, which would end with him walking away and my mother calling out my name, bending over me with worry written all over her face. But on that day, when I opened my eyes, what I saw almost made me jump out of my skin. I was inside a wheelbarrow, with Azaya pushing hard at the handles. I tried to sit up but he shouted at me to remain down. I strained my neck, looking around frantically for my mother, and sure enough she was there, running after us. . I tried to jump out of the wheelbarrow because I didn't know where he was taking me but his words stilled me,

"Ufuoma, lie down na! We dey go hospital, no worry, doctor go take care of you," Azaya yelled, in between gasps.

"Foma, no fear, I dey your back," my mother yelled behind me.

I had no other option than to lie quietly still, mortified to my bones. I could not believe I was inside a wheelbarrow! What would my classmates say if they saw me like this? The ribbing would increase for sure. There was no way I could hide because my mother was right behind me and anyone who saw her running after the wheelbarrow would know instantly that I was the one inside, as I had become quite famous because of my fainting fits.

So, I lay down still and bore the shame I felt until we got to the hospital. Azaya lifted me in his strong arms and raced inside, yelling for the doctor.

Within seconds, two nurses came out and took me from him. My mother explained everything to them while one of them took my vital signs, and the other wrote on a long sheet of paper, and then they made me sit on the hard bench in the reception. I had my mother on my right and then Isaiah came to sit on my left, so I was between the two of them.

Incredibly, I felt good. The warmth emanating from both of them was soothing. I stole a look at Brother Azaya and the worried look on his face stunned me. He seemed to really care about me and I felt humbled. None of my mother's past suitors ever showed me any concern whatsoever, and I had to admit that Brother Azaya was a good man.

"Ufuoma!" One of the nurses bellowed and I tried to get up to go meet her at her desk. I staggered and Brother Azaya quickly got up, held my hand and led me to the nurse.

"Oya, come go see, doctor." The nurse led us to the doctor›s office.

The doctor was a very large man. He seemed impatient as he glanced through my file briskly, scribbled something on it and gave it back to the nurse. The nurse led us back to the reception and asked us to sit while she prepared my drugs. After a while she called my mother aside and gave her the bill. My mother couldn't read but she held the paper close to her nose and squinted hard at it. Azaya went to her, gently took the bill from her and settled it. I stared at him in amazement. Even my late father never gave my mother any money in my presence. He never settled any bill as far as I could recall. Maybe he paid the midwife who delivered me. I could only hope so. Lost in my thoughts, I almost didn't hear when the nurse called my name again.

"Ma?" I answered and went to her.

"You don chop?" she asked.

I shook my head.

"Oya, Madam, buy coke gian make she drink because na injection I wan gian so."

Injection!

Injection? No way!!!

"Mama, I no wan take injection." I started to cry.

"You go take am if you wan well," the nurse said matter-of-factly.

"I don well, I no dey sick again," I protested.

"No worry, e no go pain you. Sister Nurse go do am small small. Oya, drink the coke." My mother urged me.

I could have protested but coke was a luxury I wouldn't pass up for the world. I only ever had it to drink on Christmas and New Year's. Never on a normal day, so I gulped everything down and belched loudly.

"Oya, come," the nurse beckoned and I started crying again, but she just laughed and called the other nurse to join my mother in holding me still.

I fought them, all the while screaming "I no go collapse again o, Mama, I no go collapse again o." My cries were to no avail as the nurse expertly jabbed at each cheek with the needles.

Meanwhile, Brother Azaya was nowhere to be found and I was happy he hadn't been there to witness my humiliation.

After my hospital visit, things changed. I stopped fainting because I didn't want a repeat of my hospital experience. I watched my mother with Azaya, and it was a whole new experience. She looked very happy because he was good to her. She never fetched firewood or water by herself anymore. He completely took over all the hard chores and left the light ones to me and my mother. Even I was happy again because he paid me attention. He helped me with my homework and told me lots of stories about places he had been.

One night, I told him about my father and how I had caused

his death and Azaya assured me that it was not my fault at all. He said that every adult is responsible for his actions and it was wrong for anyone, especially a child to be blamed for an adult's action. The next day, he took me to the herbalist's and made him retract his earlier accusation, and he did. I felt relieved afterwards because I understood finally that adults are indeed responsible for their decisions.

Brother Azaya, as my mother requested that I call him became a regular face in our house. He was always around, helping us out in one way or the other. He came mostly in the evenings, ate with us, and even helped me out with my homework. He told us lots of stories; of places he had been, people he had met, different languages, cultures, traditions and beliefs. I would stare at him, my eyes wide with amazement as he talked about Lagos. His would sound excited as he painted a scenario that made me want to run under my mother's bed in fear and at the same time want to get on the next bus to Eko, as he termed it. He was such an exciting person, and somewhat mysterious. I never got tired of his presence because I knew each visit made me more knowledgeable and enlightened about the world. Before long, the sharp ache of my father's passing began to dull. I didn't miss him that much anymore because of brother Azaya. I made a comparison between the two of them and I realized that my father had been lacking terribly in his husbandly and fatherly duties. Isaiah completely filled the space that my father left. I became more open and less timid. I became less conscious of my weaknesses and more of my strengths. My classmates used to call me ugly and I was too timid to stop them, but one day, when one of them, Voke mentioned it again, I stood up to my full height and retorted hotly:

"No! I no worwor. I fine well well. Look my eye you go see say I fine pass you sef." I charged at Voke.

And I stared her down. My eyes bright and daring had coals of fire in them and she looked shocked and frightened. Neither Voke nor the rest of my classmates had ever seen me so furious before. Voke cowered and left me alone. Everyone stopped bullying me after that. Still, I kept my distance because I didn't trust them at all.

For the first time in my life, I was at peace with myself and the people around me. I had everything I needed. I was as contented as a cat or as my people would say, "My belle just dey sweet me mion-mion."

One evening, Brother Azaya didn't show up. I stayed up late, waiting for him to come but he didn't. I asked my mother about him and she replied that he was busy. Days flew by yet there was no sign of him. I asked about him over and over again but my mother had nothing to say other than: "Broda Azaya dey busy." I searched her face, hoping to find answers but I got none.

I felt hopeless without him around. I couldn't function properly. My confidence dropped to an alarmingly low level. I didn't feel like doing anything anymore. I even played truant a couple of times and if my mother hadn't flogged the living daylights out of me when she found out, I would have continued. I started being disobedient because I believed my mother had offended Broda Azaya to make him stop coming to our house. I stopped going on errands for her and even talked back to her sometimes. My mother became worried.

I'd been exceptionally troublesome one particular day. First of all, I resisted going to school but my mother was still stronger than me, so she stood over me with a cane while I grudgingly got ready for school, murmuring all the while. She followed me all the way to school and even wanted to follow me to my class. Now, I had a reputation to maintain in school, so as we neared the gate I told her to go back.

"Foma, I must to follow you enter your class before I go go back because your head no correct dis morning," she shook her head vehemently.

"Mama, I go enter class. No worry," I maintained quietly.

Well, every mother knows her child, so at my tone she let out a deep sigh and looked at me intently.

"Foma, wetin na? Why you con change like dis na? You forget say na only you I get na?" She implored.

"What of Broda Azaya?" I spat out and I could see the surprise in her face.

"Hmmm, Foma, that matter get as e be but go your class, you hear? After, we go talk," she urged and I turned and went through the gate and straight to my class.

I could hardly concentrate all day, my mind was on the talk my mother said we would have. The hours dragged slowly and painfully by and eventually, the closing bell rang. With a sigh of relief, I threw my bag over my shoulder and moved swiftly to the door. Once I was outside, I started running all the way home. I was almost home when I realised that my mother wouldn't be home at that time. She would still be at her shed, selling. I would have gone to meet her there but she had warned me several times to never set my feet there. She said she wanted me to concentrate on my studies instead. I had to endure another long wait until she returned later that evening. I could barely contain my impatience as she took a bath, ate and did some chores. Finally, she called me to sit next to her on the long bench we had in our veranda. I sat next to her, my hands in between my thighs, waiting anxiously for what she was about to say.

"Foma, why you dey find Broda Azaya like this?"

She surprised me with her question and I tried to find an answer to it. I searched inside myself and realised then that I'd grown so fond of Azaya that living without him was something I couldn't accept. I just couldn't accept the fact that he was gone. I wanted him back. I missed him terribly. I missed his stories, I missed the care he showed us; the sense of security he gave us. I felt really miserable without him in our home. I had no idea how to convey all that to my mother.

"Mama, Broda Azaya na beta person," I answered as best as I could. "But where he con dey, Mama," I asked anxiously.

"Hmmm, he don go meet hin wife," she answered, smiling.

I was shocked. I had no idea that he had a wife. I though he wanted to make my mother his wife.

"Wife? He get wife? Mama, I be want make you be hin wife." My voice trembled and my hands shook.

Surprisingly, my mother threw back her head and laughed so hard. I didn't understand why she was laughing because I was so sad.

"Mama, why you dey laugh na?" I was angry.

"Foma ooo! Okay, make I just tell you. Broda Azaya na your brother."

And so my mother began her story. The story of how at fourteen she'd gotten pregnant for her best friend a boy two years her senior.

My mother's lover who was from a wealthy family had provided for her as best as he could. He would split his pocket money into two and give her a part. She had never even had to ask him for anything.

Ochuko, her lover had been privileged to go to school but not my mother. She'd assisted her mother in her trade, and also followed her father to the farm sometimes. Ochuko had tried many times to teach her what he learnt in school but it had been a difficult task because there had been no time as she always had one chore or the other at hand.

They had been neighbours, and as close as two peas in a pod. They had shared all they had in them with each other and their bond had grown so strong that when they had finally had sex, it hadn't seemed wrong at all. It had felt so right. And then she'd missed her period. First month. Second month. Third month. By the fourth month she could barely get up in the morning. They had both been virgins with no prior experience whatsoever.

Before my mother realized she was pregnant, her mother had noticed the changes in her body, changes she hadn't even noticed. She, who had been as thin as a rail had started to fill out. She ate and slept all the time. She threw up in the mornings and spat all day long. She had just assumed she was sick. Then her belly started to protrude.

Her mother locked her in the room one night and started questioning her. She still remembered the beating she had received that night, from both her parents. She had no choice than to confess what she had done with Ochuko, so her father, with her mother in tow had dragged her, half-naked to her lover›s house.

My mother said it had been the most traumatic and depressing experience she had ever had. She remembered the shame and pain she'd felt. Ochuko's parents had called her a prostitute, saying she wanted to pin her pregnancy on their son.

Ochuko defended her to the best of his ability, saying he was responsible for the pregnancy but he was no match for his burly father, who had beaten him to a pulp.

The two families argued and fought for weeks, unable to decide on what to do about her pregnancy. Ochuko's parents insisted that their son was not responsible for her pregnancy, while her own parents insisted that he was. So they had gone back and forth until finally the boy's parents agreed to shoulder the responsibility.

Her parents wasted no time in sending her off to Ochuko's parents' house, glad to be rid of the responsibility of catering for her. Before long, Ochuko's parents shipped him off to his mother's sister in Lagos to prevent any contact between them. She'd become some sort of a housemaid, doing all the chores, running errands and going to the market to help her mother-in-law in her trading store.

That was how it went until she delivered a baby boy who had borne a striking resemblance to Ochuko's father. That had endeared the little boy to his grandfather but after the child's second birthday, they sent my mother back to her parents' and took charge of the little boy.

"Foma, all the suffer wen I suffer no reash say I no see my Ochuko for eye again. Since dat time tina, e dey like say I no be myself. E dey like say I be pesin wen no conplete finish."

Tears ran down her face as she spoke and I felt sorry for her. She sniffed, wiped her nose with the end of her wrapper and continued her story. She had stayed at her parents' house as a stranger. Her mother had treated her like a failure, saying she hadn't even been able to extract anything tangible from her in-laws. She had decided to live each day as she saw it, and that she did until she turned thirty-two and met a man from another village who agreed to marry her. They had gotten married quickly and left the village for my father's. The following year they had me. No other children came after me so she decided to concentrate on making sure I never went hungry and that I got an education. She had worked so hard for that sole purpose.

My mother said she often thought about the child who had been forcefully taken from her, but my father had been too cowardly to help her fight to get him back. So, she had waited with confidence that he would find her one day. And he had, although she had not recognized him at first.

"Mama, how you come take know say Broda Azaya na your pikin?" I asked.

"He tell me. Dat day you come from school no meet am so? Na dat very day he tell me. And he come vex say I no find am all this time. That na why he vex comot." she explained.

"He go come back, Mama?" I asked with dread in my heart.

"I no know, my pikin," she answered in a whisper, looking far into the distance.

As the days rolled into weeks, my mother became withdrawn. She had never really been the talkative type but she became quieter, and on one occasion, when I looked closely at her face she seemed far older than before. She became a bit lax with her business. Sometimes, she would leave for the market later or return earlier than usual. I watched her every move, afraid she would fall sick as she seemed drained of energy all the time. I began to believe that telling me her story had taken a whole lot from her. I could understand that, as she had never said a word about her past to anyone. My mother had no friends that I knew of. She never, ever went visiting anyone. A neighbour had tried making friends with her a couple of times but my mother never gave her the chance, calling her: "aproko without waya."

I began to think of her one and only friend, Ochuko, the father of my brother, Azaya and it dawned on me that he probably was the only friend my mother ever had. And to think that he had been abruptly taken away from her life was a great blow for her to have survived. Then, I looked at my own life and discovered that I'd unknowingly been living my mother's life. I had no friends. None whatsoever. No one ever visited me and vice versa. I looked at my mother again and saw myself decades later. Was there still a chance for me to become what I want to become? Did I even know what I wanted to be? No, I didn't. But I knew I didn't want to end up like my mother.

After hearing my mother's story, I started making friends. It was weird at first but I slowly eased into it. I remembered how Broda Azaya had won me over by doing things I never expected him to do. By identifying my needs and seeing to them. So I employed his style. I met a few needs here and there, like helping Okiemute with his homework and before I knew it I had a host of friends. I smiled a lot too, so I became more approachable.

That done, I decided to work on getting my mother some friends. I pleaded with her to escort me to my friends' houses, and after several "Nos" she finally agreed.

We began to make friends, my mother and I. In the process

we became friends too. And as the years flew by, our friendship became stronger. She became my very best friend and I became hers. We were happy. We laughed a lot. The only thing that saddened us was the absence of Broda Azaya. We both missed him so much. Two years passed and there was no sign of him. My mother marvelled that I could grow tall, let alone beautiful because that was what I became. Tall and beautiful. At almost sixteen, I could easily pass for eighteen. The ugly duckling became a graceful swan. I indeed budded.

Broda Azaya crowded my thoughts all the time. I remembered how many times I'd wished that I had a sibling to play with. My wish came true but it was all distorted. I longed to tell him all that had happened in his absence. I longed to hear his numerous stories. I really longed to have him back in our lives.

After a while, a thought began to form in my mind. I mulled over it countless times. I had sleepless nights over it. I even prayed about it. Then, I formulated a plan. A plan to get Broda Azaya back. I knew that the realization of that plan rested in my mother's hands. One day I decided to let her in on it.

"Foma, wetin you dey talk so?" she looked up from the tray of vegetables she was picking, puzzled.

"Mama, I say make we go find Broda Azaya. We go find am go your village," I explained.

"But how you take know say he go dey there?" she asked.

"Mama, we go try first. You know say Broda Azaya vex comot say you no find am since. And you say na because Papa no get the heart to help you find am. Mama, I get the heart to help you find am, no fear. Make we go find Broda Azaya!" I said with confidence.

"Foma!" my mother stared at me and shook her head in awe. She set the tray on the floor and rose to her feet, and then with a very wide smile, she nodded in agreement.

I could barely sleep that night. My mother tossed and turned beside me, unable to sleep as well. We both gave up trying after a while, and talked instead till dawn.

My mother didn't want to go to her parents' house because she didn't want her mother to know what we were about to do, so we went straight to Brother Isaiah's grandparents' house. The house was old but I could see that it had been grand at one time. The compound was large and well swept, with a neatly trimmed lawn. My mother led me to the front door and knocked. A moment later, the door swung open to reveal an elderly woman who turned out to be Brother Isaiah's grandmother. She was shocked to see my mother; she actually looked sober but my mother gave her no hint of how she felt about the treatment she had received from them years before. She actually sounded really business-like as she enquired the whereabouts of Brother Azaya. I felt pride within me.

"Azaya don go back to Lagos. Na there he dey stay."

My heart stopped beating at her words. Even my mother's countenance fell. This place was the only place we knew to look for him.

"Where he dey stay for the Lagos? We need the address," I blurted out.

The old woman peered at me and asked, "who you be?"

"Mama, e no consine you who I be. Abeg, give us Broda Azaya's house address because we wan see am," I finally had someone to vent my anger on.

"Foma, e don do," my mother said calmly. Then she turned to the old woman and said, "Mama Ochuko, if you no give me my pikin house address now now, I go carry you take stone gran an I go gi you san san shop. E no consine me say you don old. If you let me use wetin you do me follow you, I tell you, e no go small for you. So, abeg you sofry gi mi my pikin house make I go find am," my mother had daggers in her eyes.

The woman hurried in and came out with the address written on a paper for us.

It was a new and daring adventure but we left for Lagos, in search of my brother. After a long and exciting journey, we arrived Lagos and began to search for Isaiah's house. At a point, we began to think the old woman had played a fast one on us, but eventually we stood before the house. We were surprised because the house was beautiful. Everything looked so huge; the fence, the gate. Everything. Our bravado ended, slowing down our steps. My mother drew close to the gate and knocked timidly at it.

"Foma, you sure say na Azaya house be dis?" my mother whispered to me.

"Na wetin the mama tok o. See am for the paper." I showed it to her.

"Oghene! Foma, na when I con sabi read paper na?" she asked me and we both burst into laughter. We laughed and laughed until tears rolled down our faces.

After, a while we quieted down.

"Okay, Mama wait o. Why we con dey laugh na?" I asked and we started laughing again. Then we heard loud clanging and the gate swung open to reveal Broda Azaya.

"Broda Azaya!" I screamed with joy, running into his outstretched arms.

"Oh my goodness! Ufuoma. See how tall you've grown, and beautiful too." I barely recognized his voice. It was different. A whole lot more refined. I held on to him, grinning widely.

"Mama," he said and went to my mother; our mother, and hugged her. She held him tightly, her eyes closed and her smile contented.

"What is going on here?" the deep baritone had me spinning around, toward the sound.

I heard my mother gasp as she saw the person who had spoken.

"Ochuko!" she said in disbelief.

"Mamuro," he looked shocked.

And my mother crumpled to the floor.

Broda Azaya and his father carried my mother inside the house and tried to revive her. They sprinkled water on her while I hovered around them, wringing my hands in worry. She eventually came to, to the relief of everyone and then we got settled in.

It was a wonderful reunion; the stories flowed in as both of them narrated their escapades since the last time they saw each other. We were like a family once again, aside from the fact that Azaya had a stepmother who unlike my father was very much alive and loved by Ochuko. That didn't really matter to my mother. She said she was just grateful to see him again and talk about all that happened back then. She finally had her closure.

TODAY, AS I, Ufuoma, the village joke sat in my room looking out my window at the ongoing preparations for my graduation party, I thought about my mother and the journey of our lives. I could hear my mother barking out orders to the caterers. My mother who couldn't even read had gone on to get adult education. On top of that, she found love again.

Against all odds, I went on to be the best graduating student in my class and I owed it all to brother Azaya. I met him and my life changed. He told me I was beautiful even when I thought I wasn't and I believed him and started saying it, and now people say I'm stunning.

Anything is possible. Anything can bring the change you seek. It could be something you see. Just be sure to pay attention. It could be someone you meet. For me, my turning point was meeting brother Azaya.

Getting up from the cosy love seat in my room, I strolled lazily to my closet, threw the doors open and smiled at my exquisite array of suits. Yes, come next week, I will be starting my new job with one of the top leading banks in the country. Who would have thought it possible, or according to my grandmother, "who dash monkey banana?"

### THE END

# About The Author

Ochuwa Jessica Abubakar grew up in Benin City, Edo State and studied Theatre and Media Arts at Ambrose Alli University. When she is not writing, she is baking cakes and trying to keep three little boys from burning her house down. You can interact with Ochuwa on Facebook.

# A Note from the Publisher:

Thank you for buying this collection of short stories. If you enjoyed reading it, you can help spread the word and support independent publishing by doing the following:

**Recommend it.** Suggest this book to your friends, pass it on, or buy it as a gift for someone. You can also suggest it to your book club or reader groups.

**Talk about it.** Mention it on Facebook, Instagram, Google Plus or Twitter. Create a conversation about it. You can talk about it or review it on your blog. You may also use the cover image as your profile picture on social networking sites.

**Review it.** Please leave a review online. We would appreciate genuine reviews on sites like Amazon, Smashwords and Goodreads.com

Thank you for helping us to spread the word.

**Accomplish Press**
**Find us on our: Website, Facebook and Twitter**

Manufactured by Amazon.ca
Bolton, ON